MW01137992

A SOLDIER'S TEMPTATION: EAGLE SECURITY & PROTECTION AGENCY

BEYOND VALOR BOOK 7

LYNNE ST. JAMES

A Soldier's Temptation

Copyright © 2019 by Lynne St. James
Cover Art Copyright © 2019 by Lynne St. James
Published by Coffee Bean Press
Cover by Lori Jackson Designs
Created in the United States

This book is a work of fiction. Names, characters, places, and incidents are products of the author's imagination or are used fictitiously. Any resemblance to actual events or locales or persons living, or dead is entirely coincidental.

No part of this work may be used, stored, reproduced or transmitted without written permission from the publisher except for brief quotations for review purposes as permitted by law.

This book is licensed for your personal enjoyment only and may not be re-sold or given away to other people. If you would like to share this book, please purchase an additional copy for each person.

If you're reading this book and did not purchase it, or it was not purchased for your use only, please purchase your own copy. Thank you for respecting the hard work of this author.

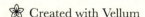 Created with Vellum

A SOLDIER'S TEMPTATION

Can he be the hero she needs?

Navy SEAL John "Riot" Dillon is finally back on track after being severely wounded and losing most of his team. Recently cleared hot and assigned to Charlie Team, he's finally getting his life back on track. It's not the best time to be attracted to his feisty neighbor, Ariana, who is in a world of trouble. But his inner-hero can't resist protecting this beautiful damsel in distress, even if she swears she doesn't need it.

After Ariana Nelson's ex-boyfriend is arrested for stealing information for the Chinese Ministry of State, her life is turned upside down.

Even in protective custody, threats against her escalate as the trial date for her ex approaches. Isolated and afraid, her sexy neighbor might be her only savior.

When the FBI drops the ball, John vows to keep Ariana safe despite her recklessness. As the danger grows, their attraction burns red hot. Will they take a chance on love before time runs out?

A Soldier's Temptation was originally published in Susan Stoker's Kindle World as *Protecting Ariana*. I've added four chapters, new characters and major story changes to this version.

DEDICATION

For T.S., my protector.

CHAPTER 1

Machine gun fire ripped through the air as SEAL Team Charlie took cover behind the shelled out husk of a building. They'd dropped into Iraqi territory at zero dark thirty to rescue a group from Doctors Without Borders. The doctors had been on their way to a refugee camp when their chopper was shot down.

After making a high altitude jump, they landed about twenty klicks from the crash site. That should have been the hard part, but from the drone surveillance, they knew the group was surrounded by enemy combatants. Now they had to get to them before it became a hostage rescue situation.

John "Riot" Dillon hated this kind of mission. Grabbing or eliminating hostiles was a lot less complicated than rescuing civilians. Most people were so freaked out they didn't know how to react and often didn't listen to the instructions which put all their safety in jeopardy.

It had been over two hours after the crash before Charlie Team was activated. Considering all they'd been through, the doctors were probably wondering if help was coming, and there'd been no way to let them know. Three and a half hours later, they were about half a klick away.

"Gus, sitrep," Elwood, their master chief requested over their coms.

"One tango on the roof watching the location of the HVTs. Two more guarding the front. It's weird they haven't moved in yet, but I don't think we have much time."

"Copy that. Do you have eyes on the civilians?"

"Negative. I can't get close enough without being seen. The windows are covered. But I have five heat signatures."

"Copy. Sit tight we're coming to you," Elwood said.

"Copy."

Gus was second in command and had taken point to scout out the HVT's location. Whoever had decided to get the doctors out of the open made an excellent decision. If they hadn't found cover, they'd be sitting ducks. They'd been shot down over one of the few areas ISIS still controlled.

"Listen up. Gus couldn't get eyes on the HVTs."

"Are we sure they're in there?" Shaggy asked. His nickname came from the cartoon as he was a dead ringer for Scooby-Doo's best bud.

"Yes, he has five hot bodies grouped together inside the building. And there are several tangos surrounding the location, it's a good call."

"What's the plan, Boss?" Disco asked. He was their medic and ballistics expert. If it needed to go boom, he made it happen.

"Shaggy, you and Riot will take out the tangos in front. Gus will take out the sniper and Disco and I will get inside and assess the situation."

"Any idea on their condition?"

"Negative. We need to be ready for anything."

"Copy that, Boss," Shaggy said.

"Worst case, we each grab one and hustle to the EXFIL," Elwood said. "We have thirty mikes to make it to the rendezvous point. Let's move."

Shaggy took point with John, Disco, and Elwood following behind. It was pitch black with the exception of occasional flashes of machine gunfire and John was happy they had NVGs. As long as they weren't shooting at the SEALs, they didn't care who they were engaging with as long as it wasn't the doctors.

As they silently made their way through the streets, they stayed in the shadows of the buildings. It should ensure that if anyone was searching for them, they'd be a lot harder to spot.

"Elwood, we have movement," Gus' voice echoed in their earpieces.

"Copy that. We're within range. Are there more tangos?"

"Two more just showed up. Not sure if they're relieving the others or not."

"Copy that. We're on your six. Get ready to

take out the sniper. We've got the others," Elwood replied.

"Copy."

"Go on my signal," Elwood told the rest of the team.

John and Shaggy took their position on the side of the building closer to where the HVTs were located. They'd need to move quickly to take out all four tangos before they got off a shot and alerted anyone in the area.

Pulling out their ka-bars, Shaggy and John waited for the signal. It came a few heartbeats later.

"Go."

The burst of adrenaline never got old for John, and he surged toward the ISIS soldiers. Before they realized what was happening, they'd sliced their throats and pulled them into the shadows. Gus took out the sniper on the roof with the same precision.

After verifying the area was clear, they entered the building. Disco was tending to a woman lying on a table and Elwood was deep in discussion with a tall grey-haired guy. As they entered, he looked up and nodded.

The doctors weren't in bad shape considering they'd been in a chopper crash, walked about two klicks, and spent the last few hours hoping they'd be rescued. He'd expected a group of blood-covered, moaning people but then again they were doctors.

John joined Disco at the table. "Do you need help with anything?"

"I'm giving everyone a shot of antibiotics. Their supplies were destroyed in the crash, but they managed to do decent triage on each other."

"We *are* doctors," the woman said as she rolled down her sleeve from receiving the injection.

"Yes, ma'am. I didn't mean anything by it."

"I'm sorry. It's been a rough few hours."

"No worries, we're here now and soon you'll be out of here," John said, hoping they'd be able to move them to the EXFIL point without incident.

"Thank you. We really do appreciate you coming for us. We didn't know if anyone heard our SOS. The longer we waited, the more panicked everyone got thinking we were on our own. I'm Dr. Alicia Thompson by the way."

"I'm Riot and he's Disco. The call was

picked up and we came as soon as we could," John answered.

"Do I want to know how you got those names?" Dr. Thompson asked.

"Probably not," Disco answered with a smile. "You're all set."

"Thanks."

After Disco packed his gear they joined Elwood. They had about thirty mikes to make it to the EXFIL point unless something changed.

"Status?" Elwood asked Disco.

"Mostly cuts and scrapes, two possible concussions, a broken arm, and a broken ankle. All say they're mobile."

"Okay, you take the broken ankle, the rest of you paid off. The HELO is inbound."

"Copy," they replied in unison.

"Can I have everyone's attention?"

The group grew quiet and turned toward Elwood.

"We have ten minutes to make it where the helicopter will pick us up. We have to move quickly. If you can't walk, tell us now and we'll carry you. We do it all the time. No shame in it at all and it's better to tell us now than hold everyone up," Elwood announced as he looked at each of the group.

Two people raised their hands, the guy with the broken ankle, and a woman he hadn't spoken to yet. Disco took the broken ankle as ordered, and John went to grab the woman.

"I've got you, ma'am. I'm Riot and I'll be your transport. Just hold on tight and it'll be fine," John said as he lifted her into his arms.

"Thank you, Riot. My name is Jeannie, I'm one of the nurses."

"Nice to meet you. We'll get you out of here and back home in no time."

"But we're not going home," Jeannie said.

Frustrating but not unexpected. You didn't become a part of Doctors Without Borders without tempering your stubborn streak. Hopefully, they wouldn't have to come back and rescue them again.

In the end, only two of the group was able to walk. The SEALs carried the others. They had a lot of ground to cover in a short period of time. The last thing they needed was the rescue to turn into a clusterfuck. John had been in that position once before and it was enough.

Prior to joining Charlie Team, he'd been a

member of Tango Team, but most of his team-mates had been killed in action. Only John and his Senior Master Chief Chase "Frost" Brennan survived. In a less than a blink of an eye, all hell broke loose as they approached the target. Surrounded by the enemy, broken and bleeding, it was a miracle they'd remained alive and undiscovered until the Marines found them a few hours later.

Reminiscing put him in a bad headspace. It had taken almost a year of rehab and psych evals before he was cleared to operate. Joining Charlie Team gave him a second chance at the life he'd always wanted. Concentrating on the woman in his arms and getting to the EXFIL point was all that mattered.

As the chopper landed in the distance, shots rang out behind them.

"Get to the EXFIL. Shaggy and I will cut them off," Elwood commanded through their coms.

Picking up the pace, he ran faster toward the rendezvous point. They were almost there.

"Not much longer, Jeannie," John said. As soon as the gunshots started, she'd tensed up and begun shaking. "It'll be okay."

"Thank you," her voice was shaky and tear-filled.

He didn't know how else to comfort her, except to get her onto the helicopter. Gus and Disco were even with him as they sprinted toward where it landed. They helped the three they'd been carrying into the chopper, then assisted the other two. Once they were settled, Gus and John ran back to help their teammates. Disco stayed behind to check the status of the injured.

"We'll be right back, two of the team is still out there," Gus yelled to one of the marines on the HELO.

As the gunfire continued to shred the darkness, Gus and John ran toward the sound. Before they could get there, Elwood and Shaggy ran out of the tree line. A few minutes later they were airborne, and everyone was alive. There would be beers all around when they got back to base. This was a huge win.

After landing at Bagram Air Base, the Doctors without Borders group was taken to the hospital for further evaluation. Charlie Team stopped at the TOC to give the after-action report. Their three-month deployment was finally over. Hopefully, it would be the last one for a while.

Unless something else came up before the replacement team arrived, they were headed home in the morning. Or later that day actually since it was almost dawn. They'd been deployed for the last three months. John was more than ready to get back home to Coronado. And Ariana.

Who was he kidding? There hadn't been a moment of downtime that he hadn't been worried about her. Or daydreaming was more like it. He'd met his neighbor, Ariana Nelson, shortly after he'd moved into the building. The attraction had been instant from the first time he'd spoken to her. Later, he found out that she was in a world of shit.

His old college roommate and FBI agent, Colin Rogers, asked him if he could help keep an eye on her while he was on medical leave. He'd been happy to do it and hoped that seeing her in a different light would help kill his attraction, instead it grew.

After he'd gotten cleared hot and assigned

to Charlie Team, it had been hard to leave her, knowing she was in danger. The timing of their deployment sucked, but he'd made Colin give him updates on how she was doing. He was really looking forward to getting home and seeing her again.

"You thinking about that woman again?" Gus asked.

"Woman? Nah, just thinking about getting out of this sandy hell hole," John replied, hoping they'd believe him. He was over their teasing about Ari. It had been a mistake to tell them about her.

"Sure, you were," Shaggy said. "You have that lovesick look on your face again."

"I'm not lovesick. Just concerned about her safety. It's what we do, right? Protect people?"

"When's the trial?" Elwood asked.

"Not sure. It could have already happened. Colin doesn't give me a lot of details, I have to drag information out of him," John answered.

"She might have taken the WITSEC option too," Shaggy said.

"I doubt it, she was adamant about not giving up her life. That took a lot of guts."

"It did, but like you said, who knows what's

happened since you've been here," Disco agreed.

"I guess I'll find out soon enough. Unless we're not going home today?" John asked looking at Elwood.

"Nope, we're out of here. Transport departs at zero ten-thirty. And don't forget to leave your love letters for Echo Team," Elwood said with a grin.

It was a tradition to write letters for the next deployed team. Some of them were freakin' hysterical. Over the years, John had saved a couple he'd received. After writing a quick note and leaving it on the desk, he tried to focus on packing. But he couldn't get Ari out of his head. He'd lose his shit if she went into WITSEC, even if it was the safest place for her.

The extent of their relationship, if you could call it that, were a few conversations in the gym and when he stopped by to pick up his plant. As much as he'd wanted to, he'd never kissed or even touched her. It was the complete opposite of how he usually was with women. But since he'd been wounded, he'd changed more than physically. Having to answer a lot of questions about the scars covering most of his body was a total mood killer. It hadn't been worth the effort. Until he met Ari. She was the first woman he'd had a physical reaction to in months.

"Are you just going to stand there or start packing? Maybe you want to stay after all?" Gus asked with a smile.

"Oh hell no. I can't wait to get home and have a decent shower," he replied. It was true too. Besides Ari, he missed his shower the most.

CHAPTER 2

"Is he always this potent?"

"What?" Ariana knew exactly what her BFF Shira meant, but she wanted to hear her say it.

"You don't smell the stank that's coming from that fuzzy menace?"

"Are you referring to Mr. Darcy?"

"You know Jane Austin is spinning in her grave, right? Seriously, Sir Fartsalot would be a more appropriate name."

"It's not that bad."

"Are you shitting me? How do you live with him? I swear it's been one silent but deadly cloud after another since I got here."

The scrunched-up expression on Shira's face as she tried to avoid sucking in the contaminated air was priceless. If Ari had more guts, she'd snap a picture and put it on Instagram, but she'd be dead if she tried.

"He's not usually like this. I think it's the flea meds the vet gave him or maybe the new food."

As if he knew what they were talking about, Mr. Darcy stood up from where he'd been lying at Ari's feet and spun around to release another silent bomb in Shira's direction. It was all she could do not to bust out laughing as Shira's eyes almost bugged out of her face.

"You need to do something about that. It's horrible. How the hell are you going to hook a guy if you have this fart factory living with you?"

"I'm not looking for a guy."

"You should be. And you want to tell me again why you felt the need to adopt a dog?"

Ari sighed. They had this conversation every time Shira visited her apartment. She was a cat person and no matter how adorable Mr. Darcy was, she'd never like him, stink or not. "I love him. He needed me, and I needed him."

"Ugh. You should have adopted a cat."

"I didn't want a cat. They won't cuddle or share popcorn."

"See, this is what I've been telling you. You need to start dating again, find a man, and get rid of the fuzzy fart machine. The dirtbag who shall not be named has been out of your life for over a year. It's time to move on."

"I'm happy. I have moved on, but it doesn't mean I need to find someone else. It hasn't been that long."

"That's what you keep telling me. Yet you always find an excuse not to come out with us. At this rate, you will end up alone with stinky butt."

"I'm thirty years old, I don't want a one-night-stand which is all I'd find at that SEAL bar you hang out in. I want a relationship some-day, but not yet, and I'm not sure it's even possible."

"Of course, it's possible. But you won't know until you try."

Ari took a sip of her coffee as Shira's words sank in. Subconsciously, she reached down and slid her fingers through the soft-kinky fur on Mr. Darcy's head. He nuzzled against her hand.

"You know I'm right."

"Maybe. But I have trust issues."

"Considering what that fucktard did…"

"He wasn't like that in the beginning. He was so charming. You even liked him."

"I did, but Paul Chen is a con artist. Maybe not in the typical sense, he tricked you into dating him so he could steal information from your computer, didn't he?"

"Yes, and that's the problem. I almost ended up in prison for the rest of my life because of my bad judgment when it came to him. If the FBI hadn't found the other computer he'd hidden, I would still be in jail."

"Thankfully, they figured that shit out before it happened."

"Yeah, but it's still hard. I think everyone I meet has an ulterior motive. Not that there have been a lot of new people in my life. The FBI has seen to that."

"But if you don't take a chance you'll never know. You have to put yourself out there."

It's not like Ari wasn't attracted to anyone. Her gorgeous neighbor occupied most of her fantasies and she would have considered dating him. Then she found out he was a Navy SEAL. She wanted a real relationship, someone who would be willing to invest time in her and prove himself, not a one night stand.

Shira rolled her eyes. Ari knew what was coming, but she was saved by a knock on the door.

"Who's that?"

"Umm, last I checked I don't have x-ray vision." Ari laughed as she went to answer the door. A keycard was required to access the building, so it had to be one of her neighbors, probably Mrs. Laramie the sweet elderly woman how brought her cookies whenever she baked.

"I can't believe you opened the door without looking. What did I tell you about checking first?"

"Hi, John. Nice to see you, too." Ari stepped back so she could look up into the face of the man who fueled her fantasies. He'd moved in shortly after her and lived down the hall.

"Don't you watch the news? Read the papers? The internet? You need to check before you open the door, anyone could be on the other side."

"But you need a key to get into the building or know the code."

"Yeah, and no one could get around that,

right? Promise me you'll check before you open the door from now on."

"How do you know I didn't?"

"I heard you. It's what I do, remember?" he said with a smile. God, he was drop-dead sexy.

"Welcome back. I'm sure Miss Jade missed you."

"Thanks. But I don't think she'd know whether I'm here or not as long as she has light and water. Maybe I should just leave her here, she spends more time with you than at my place."

Before Ari could answer, Shira appeared at her side.

"Hi, I'm Shira, Ari's best friend. She's been holding out on me," she said as her eyes traveled his body.

Apparently, wishing for a hole to open up on the floor and suck her in wasn't in the cards. She'd been so engrossed in John's emerald-green eyes she'd forgotten all about Shira and Mr. Darcy, who chose that moment to release a stink bomb.

Ari apologized for her fuzzy companion's lack of decorum.

John laughed. "You finally brought him home, huh?"

"Yeah, they approved the adoption after you left." Ari didn't have to see Shira's face to know what she was thinking and had to put the brakes on it as soon as possible. "Shira, this is John. He lives down the hall, and I babysit his plant when he goes out of town."

"I see."

"Hi, Shira. Nice to meet you."

"Same here. Why don't you come in? We're having coffee, and I brought some delicious cookies. Unless the fuzzy gasbag is too much."

"Nothing could be worse than being stuck in a tent with a bunch of guys eating MREs. Nothing that dog can do could top that. Unfortunately, I'll have to take a raincheck. I just got back, and I'm beat."

Ari tried to hide her sigh of relief. The last thing she needed was Shira grilling John. Her *interrogation* would be bad enough without him there. "Let me get Miss Jade." Quickly going to the coffee table, she grabbed his plant and handed it to him.

"I watered her this morning, so she should be good for a few days."

"Great, thank you. I really appreciate you taking care of her while I'm gone. It was nice meeting you, Shira. Have fun. I'll catch you later, Ariana."

Then he was gone, the sunshine seemed to dim a bit as she shut the door and turned to face her smirking friend. Oh yeah, she had it bad. He was part of the reason Ari didn't date. No one could compare to John Dillon. She'd been drawn to him since the first time they spoke. He was so down to earth it was hard to believe he was a big bad Navy SEAL.

Over the last few months, they'd gotten to know each other better, but he'd never made a move. In all fairness, she'd never done anything to further the relationship either. After the disaster with her ex, Paul, she didn't know if she wanted to take another chance. Besides, as far as she could tell he just considered her his plant sitter.

"John, huh? You've been holding out on me."

"Nope."

"Mr. tall dark and handsome lives down the hall and you never told me about him? And you babysit his plant?"

"There's nothing to tell. We met at the gym, and he gave me some pointers."

"I just bet he gave you some pointers," Shira answered her expression showing exactly what she thought about his help.

"Stop that. You make everything sound dirty. He showed me how to lift without hurting myself."

"Lift? Since when did you start lifting weights? Girl, is this why you won't go out with us? You're too busy 'working out' with Mr. Six-pack down the hall?"

"See, this is exactly why I didn't tell you about him. We're friends. That's it. Got it?"

"Uh huh, sure. Just friends. So, have you and your new friend been out for coffee yet?"

"No. No coffee, no dinner, no dating. I told you, I have no desire to get involved again. Paul was enough to last me a lifetime."

"Your lips are saying one thing, but I saw your face when you were talking to him. Girl-friend, you have it bad." This was exactly why Ari hadn't mentioned John to Shira. She was her best friend, but once she got an idea in her head she latched onto it like a vice grip, and it was game over. Except John was no game. Ari couldn't imagine any scenario where it would work out, so she wasn't going to take the chance.

"Can we change the subject? I really, really don't want to talk about John."

"Fine, but this conversation isn't closed. I want to know all about him, and what's the deal with the plant?"

"If I tell you about the plant can we drop the subject?"

"Sure. For today. There's no way I'm letting you blow off that gorgeous hunk of manhood. Unless you're really not interested, because then I'll take a shot at him."

"Don't even think about it."

"Uh huh, I thought so. Okay, so what's the deal with the plant?"

As if to add his two cents, Mr. Darcy released a gaseous cloud in Shira's direction before heading into the kitchen. Maybe that was the solution, if Ari could get Mr. Darcy to fart on command, she could end countless conversations she didn't want to have. Just thinking about it made her giggle which didn't go unnoticed by Shira who had her face half-buried in her shirt to avoid the smell.

"C'mon, it's not that bad."

"You're shitting me, right? It's horrific. How do you live like this?"

Now Ari did giggle. It *was* pretty bad, but she'd never admit it to Shira. It really was worse than usual. Maybe Mr. Darcy had gotten into something he shouldn't have.

"Do you want to go onto the balcony?"

"If you leave Mr. Farty inside."

"It's Mr. Darcy. You're going to hurt his feelings."

"Now I know you've lost it," Shira said as she grabbed her coffee mug and the plate of cookies. Ari followed with her coffee. "Ahh, fresh air. I can breathe again."

"You act like cats don't smell up the place. What about the litter box?"

"I have that automated one. It never stinks, and you know it."

"If you say so." Shira was right, her apartment never smelled like a litter box, but she had to do something to defend her precious Mr. Darcy. It wasn't his fault he had a sensitive stomach.

"Okay, you've stalled long enough. What's

the deal with the plant? You called it what? Miss Jade? He named his plant? And since he's away all the time, why get a plant anyway?"

"No, not exactly. I named her. And don't give me that look, you know I always name everything. I figured if I was going to watch her she should have a name."

"But it's a plant. And that still doesn't explain why someone who knows he's going to be away more than at home would get a plant. I think he did it to meet you."

"Oh my God, you're such a brat. Do you hear yourself? He didn't get the plant to meet me. And it's not a big deal I talk to them. It helps them thrive. Don't you talk to yours?"

"No. And why didn't I know you do? You were never like this until you moved in with 'he who must not be named.' I blame him."

Ari shrugged. She was right, she'd changed after the mess with Paul. She still had night-mares over what went down with the FBI. But at least they knew she wasn't guilty of anything. After he was arrested, she'd moved into this apartment to get a new start. It was a nice place, but it was the first time she'd lived alone. Even after ten months, she still hadn't gotten used to it, which is why she got Mr. Darcy. "Does it matter?"

"Are you losing your mind?"

"No, I'm as sane as you are."

"Maybe." But she softened her words with a grin. They'd been friends forever, and Ari knew Shira was right. Over the last year, she'd become a hermit, staying home and avoiding everyone. It's no wonder she was worried about her.

"I'm sorry. I know it's been weird. But after all the crap with you know who, I figured I'd give myself a chance to get over it. Lick my wounds. You know?"

"Girl, I do know. The rat bastard put you through hell. But you need to remember you're not alone. I love you and worry about you. I want my old Ari back. You've changed so much. We used to share everything. Now I don't even know that you talk to plants and have a super-hottie living down the hall. I guess I should be happy you told me you were adopting the four-legged gasbag before you did."

"Yes, you should." Shira was right, Ari

hadn't been as open with her. She was lucky she hadn't given up on her. But until she was sure anyone around her wasn't at risk, she had to keep them at a distance. Even though doing it made her feel sad and isolated. The only people she saw were at work, and even they kept their distance.

"You need to get out more. Being cooped up isn't good for you."

"I'm not *cooped up*. I still go to work."

"That doesn't count. I miss you. Having coffee once a month isn't enough."

"I'm sorry."

"Then do something about it. You used to love dancing. I'm sure if you come out with us you'll have a great time. Unless you're secretly dating Mr. Hot Stuff?"

Ari rolled her eyes. Shira wasn't going to let up on John no matter how much she wanted her to drop it. "I don't like to leave Mr. Darcy. He's alone all day while I'm at work."

"You've only had the dog for about a month. What's your excuse for the eight months before that?"

"You already know the reason. I don't feel safe."

"But you have those guys protecting you."

"And if something happens then whoever I'm around is in danger too. It's just easier to stay at home. Besides, think about all the questions I'd have to answer about why they're following me. No thank you."

The newspapers had covered her arrest and then Paul's. She'd gone from an anonymous person who was living her best life, to front-page news and it had been horrible. She'd had to change her phone number and try to disguise herself when she went out to get groceries.

The first few months afterward were the worst and she wasn't even allowed back to work. It took three months for her to get cleared to return to work. Even then her top secret projects were reassigned. It took another six months before she finally got her clearance back, but she still felt the stares at meetings.

"Come out with us tomorrow night. There's a new band playing at the club."

"Which club?

Shira rolled her eyes. "You know which one."

"I told you I don't want to hang around and be SEAL-bait."

"Why don't you bring John? No one would dream of hitting on you with that hunk hanging around."

"And subject him to all of you? Are you crazy? He'd never talk to me again. Besides, we're just friends actually more like acquaintances."

"Whatever. Why not ask him? It couldn't hurt and he might even say yes."

"I'll think about it."

"You're afraid he'll say yes, aren't you?"

"You know you're a stubborn woman, right?"

"Yup. You tell me at least once a week."

Ari grinned. It was true. But she'd rather be stubborn and stand up for herself than be a doormat like some of the women they used to try to help when they were in college.

"I've got to get going. Promise me you'll think about coming with us?"

"I promise." Ari hugged Shira as they got to the front door. "Thanks for bringing the yummy cookies."

"Too bad they were contaminated by Mr. Stink Bomb."

"You need to let that go," Ari said as she laughed and rubbed Mr. Darcy's head. Then she bent down so he could give her a kiss. She loved her stinky dog more than anything.

"Ugh, dog germs. I can't believe you let him lick your face. And I'm not letting it go until he quits contaminating everything. You need to figure out what his problem is or put a bag on his ass to catch the stink."

Ari burst out laughing. Thinking about her fuzzy baby walking around with a bag on his butt was too much. Soon they were both laughing like they used to, and all the other stuff was forgotten.

"I love you, girl. I promise to try to be better," Ari said as she hugged Shira tightly. She was her oldest and best friend, and they'd always been there for each other. As much as she missed her, it was safer this way. There was just too much danger in Ari's life right now.

"I love you too. Talk to you soon," Shira said with a smile. "I'm going to call you and remind you about the club."

"Okay," Ari said as she closed the door behind her friend with a sigh. Shira filled the apartment with life and she always felt extra alone after she went home. Thank God for Mr. Darcy.

After gathering the dirty dishes and putting the cookies away, Ari went to her desk to do her journaling. Another thing she hadn't shared with Shira yet. The FBI had asked her to write down everything she could remember about Paul in as much detail as possible. They wanted to make sure she'd be ready and not forgotten anything when she had to testify.

That's how it started, but after she'd written everything she could remember, she kept going. It morphed into a brain dump, and soon it became a daily habit of writing down her thoughts, worries, hopes, and dreams.

A notification ding from her phone pulled her attention away from the journal. It was a new email. Recognizing the name, the blood rushed out of her head and the room spun. It was crazy that after a year just seeing his name made her break out in a cold sweat and want to burst into tears.

He wasn't supposed to have internet access, so how had he sent her an email from prison? Unless it wasn't him? If she hadn't been sitting, she'd probably have fallen over. Seeing his name was bad enough, but when she opened the email blind panic set in.

There were no words, just a photo of her and Shira sitting on the balcony with a big red "X" over Shira's face. It didn't take a rocket scientist to know what it implied. Shaking, she tried to take a deep breath, but it only made it worse. This was her worst nightmare and what she'd been trying to prevent. Was anyone in her life safe? With no clue what else to do, she called Colin, the FBI agent. Hopefully, he'd have some answers.

When she finally got ahold of Colin, he told her that he'd have the IT department remote into her computer and see what they could find.

"It's just more scare tactics like I told you they'd try. They're going to do everything they can to try to keep you from testifying."

"You don't think Shira is in danger?"

"No, I don't. But if you'd go into WITSEC you wouldn't have to worry about any of this."

"And I'd lose everyone I love. No thank you."

"Okay, but I did warn you. If you get

scared, grab the agent downstairs and he can come to stay with you."

"It's okay. Just try to find out who's behind this."

"We will. I'll check on you tomorrow."

CHAPTER 3

Carrying "Miss Jade" into his apartment, John caught a glimpse of his face in the mirror. Damn, smiling like a jackass again. The woman was like a burst of sunshine whenever he saw her. Trying to stay neighborly and not take it further seemed to get harder each time he looked into her aquamarine eyes.

During the last mission, Gus and Disco gave him a rash of shit for mooning about some woman, that he looked like some kind of a lovesick puppy. Lovesick? Who the fuck even said that anymore. It didn't matter how much he denied it, they were taking bets on how long it would take him to settle down.

Crazy. Yup, that's what they were. SEALs didn't do well in long-term relationships. Elwood reminded him about his friend Rafe on the Black Eagle team. His woman had been involved in a mission too. What were the odds of that? Could he do that to a woman he loved? Leave her behind with the chance of never coming back? It had been a close call last time, only he and Frost had made it back alive. It was a moot point, getting involved with Ariana wasn't an option. He was just helping out a buddy and trying to keep her safe.

Hell, just thinking about how she'd react when she found out the truth was almost enough to make him back off, almost. At first, he'd felt guilty about using the plant to get closer to her, but it was nothing compared to what he was really hiding. John was trustworthy. He was a freakin' Navy SEAL, and that had to count for something. Hopefully, enough of a something for her to forgive him for the ruse.

A lot of downtime before being assigned to Charlie Team gave him time to keep an eye on Ariana. He'd bumped into her a few times and been intrigued when he'd seen her working out in the building's gym. That was before it became an assignment. He'd been watching her for months and knew all about her friend Shira Redmond, this was the first time he'd met her.

When FBI Agent Colin Rogers, his former college roommate, asked for some unofficial help with a witness who refused Witness Protection he'd been intrigued. According to Colin, most jumped at the chance for a new life, but not Ariana Nelson.

Waiting had been driving him crazy. Patience was not one of his virtues and even doing PT daily wasn't enough to keep him from climbing the walls with boredom. The recertification process took time for a reason, but he didn't want to hear it. His body was healed, and he'd passed all the tests. Waiting for the official word had sucked.

The notification that he'd been cleared, good to go by medical couldn't have made him happier. He'd just about given up on ever getting back on the Teams. He'd even considered his ex-chief's job offer. Chase Brennan, Frost when he was on the Teams, ran the Eagle Security & Protection Agency in Florida. John had no real ties to California other than his friends on the Teams so it would have been easy enough to move. But he wasn't ready to give up being a frogman. It was all he'd ever wanted.

Now that he was back to work and assigned to Charlie Team it felt like he was back where he belonged. Except for Ariana. When he was off on a mission he worried that something would happen without him to watch out for her. Colin put someone else on the job. But even though at that point he'd never spoken to her, he wasn't ready to give up on his damsel in distress. Needing a reason to talk to her, check on her, make sure she was safe, had become a part of his life.

The plant seemed like the perfect solution at the time. He'd been toast the first time he'd spoken to her at the gym. He didn't need the facilities, he had better equipment on base, but it was the least threatening way he could think to approach her.

Ariana was funny, smart, stubborn as nails, and unlike any of the women he usually dated. Without even realizing it, the prickly little ball of fire had stolen his heart. He tried to tell himself it was brotherly concern at first. Yeah, no. That worked for about ten seconds. He was supposed to be a professional. Falling for his 'assignment' was not an option.

There was nothing he could do about any of it now, it would have to play out, and he hoped like hell Ariana would understand when she found out the truth. With a sigh, he grabbed a beer from the refrigerator and dropped onto the sofa to see if there was a game on. As he channel surfed, his cell phone rang.

"Hey, Colin. How's it going?" Gotta love caller ID. How had they lived without it?

"Good. I heard you were back."

"How did you…oh never mind. But damn, if I'm on a top-secret mission overseas I don't want to know how you find out this stuff."

"Let's just say that because of our girl I know more than I should."

"Ariana? I just saw her, she seemed fine. She's even got a dog now."

"She's not fine. She got an email that spooked her bad. I'm on my way to her place."

"Do you want me to stop by?"

"No. It's why I'm calling, to give you the heads up that I'll be there so we don't bump into each other."

"Why don't you let me go over there

instead? I still think we should just level with her. What harm could it do to let her know I've been watching out for her?" John prayed he'd say yes, although he already knew the answer. The freakin' FBI was as bad as the CIA and never shared anything until they had to. But he didn't work for them, this was off-book, and techni-cally Colin couldn't do a damn thing if he told Ariana.

"Are you really asking me that? We still need to figure out who else is involved. He had at least one accomplice, and we need to smoke them out."

"Okay, I get it, but you're an FBI agent. Don't you think they know who you are? I'm just a guy that's been hanging around her. And for the record, I'm not going to lie to her forever."

"You're not lying, you're protecting her. And, you're supposed to be off the case. You're only still involved because you want to be, and you should just leave it to us. I have two guys on her. Once you went back on active duty, you were done. I could lose my badge for this. I shouldn't have involved you, but we didn't think she would be in danger, so it was more like a precaution."

"Fine. I'll keep it quiet for now. But I won't stop checking on her when I'm home. I like her."

"You forget I lived with you for four years and you sniff out trouble like a bloodhound. I know how you are. Do yourself a favor and don't fall for her. I'm still hoping we can get her into WITSEC. Even after Chen's trial, she won't be safe, especially if we can't find the other bad actors involved."

"Don't worry about me, I can take care of myself. But I really think I should be the one to go see her now."

"I'm already in the parking lot. Besides, they'd expect her to call me. It would be odd if you went back after just being there. I'll let you know when I have more. Later."

Colin was a pain in his ass, but that was part of what made him an excellent agent. He'd moved up through the ranks faster than anyone else in his class at Quantico. If he didn't love working in the field so much, he'd be a supervisor. John understood the thrill of the hunt.

Too antsy to watch TV, John took his beer onto the balcony. He wasn't close enough to see Ariana's apartment, but he checked out the area. It made him feel a little better. Chen's trial was supposed to happen in a week. He'd expected an escalation of trouble before now. Whoever was involved had done the usual crap: hang-ups, untraceable email threats, and slashed tires. Ariana had been strong through all of it, until now. What had spooked in that email? It was eating him up inside not being there to make sure she was okay.

Tired from the mission and frustrated about Ariana did not make a good combination. Grabbing another beer from the fridge he sat on the balcony. Maybe Colin was right, maybe he needed to back off. Just because he was attracted to her didn't mean the feeling was mutual. Chen had put her through hell, still was. He wouldn't be surprised if she'd never trust another man.

John tried to relax, forget about it, but when he still hadn't heard from Colin he was ready to say fuck it and go to Ariana's apartment. It took sixty-six minutes before he heard from Colin. His training prepared him for waiting, but this was different. This was personal whether he liked it or not. Pacing back and forth between the balcony and the living room, he only stopped long enough to take a detour for another bottle of beer. He'd been so intent on watching the time and imagining the worst, that when his pocket vibrated he almost dropped his beer.

"You took your sweet time."

"Didn't have much choice. We have a situation."

"Is she okay?"

"Depends on what you mean by okay. Physically, yes. Mentally, she's a wreck. The sonofabitches sent her threatening pictures."

"Fuck. What kind of threats?"

"Pictures of her sitting on the balcony with her girlfriend. She's terrified that because of her something will happen to her friend."

"If you were in her shoes, you'd be too."

"Maybe, but we're trained for this. And dammit if she'd go into WITSEC she wouldn't have to worry about this. Hell, we wouldn't have to worry about this. She'd be the Marshalls problem."

"That's bullshit, and you know it. She'd be safe, but her friends wouldn't be. I know you're trying to do your job, but you need to remember these are people with real lives. I think you've forgotten that."

"Shut the hell up. You don't know what the fuck you're talking about, and I'm not about to go into it now. One of these nights it'll be you, me, and a bottle of tequila, and I'll explain. In the meantime, the best way to protect her would be a safe house, but I can't get her to agree to that either. She's worried if she disappears they'll go after her friend. I told her we'd keep watch over her friends too."

"She said no."

"Give the man a beer."

"Fuck."

"There is another option. How close are you two?"

"What do you mean?"

"Listen, John, don't try to shit me. You're a great guy but you've gone way over and above keeping watch over her. She's not your responsibility, yet you won't back off. Did you forget we have her under surveillance?"

"What does that have to do with anything? Oh yeah, and your guy is an amateur. I spotted him right away from my window. You need to put someone else on her."

"No, he's not, those were his orders. We figured if it was obvious she had protection they'd back off."

"How's that working out for you?"

"Smartass. Do you think you can convince Ariana to go to a safe house?"

"Probably not. She hasn't opened up to me at all. As far as I can tell she hasn't told her friends either."

Colin's sigh was more exasperation and it came through the phone loud and clear. John understood. He'd been on missions where no matter how hard you tried to protect someone they did everything they could to fight you. He'd have to do something, he needed her in a safe place. The question was how to go about it.

"Let me see what I can do. I've been dropping hints that I'm interested, but so far she's been oblivious."

"Holy shit. Riot the heartthrob is striking out?"

"You don't want to go there, trust me. I've been taking it slow. I didn't want to scare her away. Besides, it feels wrong since she thinks I'm someone I'm not."

"Not true. You're a Navy SEAL, you told her that, right?"

"Yeah."

"Then you're exactly who you said you are. The only thing you're not copping to is that you volunteered to help keep her safe. I don't see how she could be upset."

"You don't have a girlfriend, do you?"

"What does that have to do with anything?"

"If you did, you wouldn't ask. I'll do my best."

"Thanks. I'll call you after I get some more answers. Be careful. If they're watching her, they're watching you too."

After he hung up with Colin, he jumped into the shower. Water always helped him think more clearly, probably part of the reason he functioned so well as a SEAL. By the time he was done, he'd put together a plan. Now to see if it would work.

Standing outside the door of Ariana's apartment, John debated the odds. He'd thought about calling first, but decided he had a better chance of her saying yes if she had to look him in the face. It never hurt to play on one's strengths. Of course, his strengths weren't the same after he'd been nearly blown to bits almost two years ago.

Dressed for success, as his mother used to say, he hoped she'd take him up on his offer. But first, he needed to knock on the door. Why was he nervous? It's not like this was a date even if it felt like one. He was in protection mode. Getting involved with this woman was a mistake, his brain knew it even if his heart didn't want to hear about it.

The knock brought her to the door. Hearing the patter of Mr. Darcy's paws on the wood floors, he waited to see if she'd look through the peephole before opening the door.

She'd checked, like he asked, the earlier scare probably had something to do with it. What he hadn't expected was her quivering smile and tear-reddened eyes. She didn't look like the same woman he'd spoken to a couple of hours ago.

"Are you okay? Did something happen?"

"Yeah, no, I don't know. Umm, do you want to come in? Did you need something?"

John stepped through the door and closed it behind him, making sure it was locked and bolted. "Did something happen with your friend?" He hated not being able to fess up about what he already knew. It would make it so much easier.

"No, nothing like that. It's something else. Anyway, I'm fine. What's up? Do you have to leave again?"

"No, not yet. Hopefully, we have a few weeks before we head out again. Actually, I was hoping you'd have dinner with me. My fridge is empty except for beer, and I don't feel like fast food."

"Umm, I don't know…" Ari hadn't met his eyes since she'd answered the door. He hated seeing her like this. There was no way he would let those bastards harm a hair on her head.

"C'mon. It will be good to get out for a bit, no?"

"What about Mr. Darcy? I don't like to leave him alone."

John had been prepared for that argument. "No problem. I want to try that little Italian bistro down the street. They have tables outside, and I've seen other people who'd brought their dogs when dining. Have you been there?"

"Do you mean Amici's?"

"Yup that's it. You can't tell me that a nice glass of red wine and a piece of lasagna doesn't make your mouth water?"

He had her, he knew it, she knew it, and he had a feeling even Mr. Darcy knew it. His tail was wagging like crazy. "C'mon. You know you want to."

Mr. Darcy pushed his head into her hand as if he was adding his two cents. He'd have to remember to get that dog a treat the next time he was at the store.

"Are you sure you want to eat outside?"

"Oh yeah. I did it all the time when I was in New York and ate in Little Italy. It's cool to people watch and enjoy a great dinner. It's even better when you have a beautiful woman to do it with."

She didn't answer at first but then said, "Are you flirting with me?"

"Maybe a little. I'm willing to try anything."

He was ready for her to turn him down, but instead, she surprised him again.

"Alright. Give me about ten minutes to get ready, okay? Do you want to wait here, or I can meet you downstairs?"

"I'll wait if you don't mind?"

"Sure. Mr. Darcy will keep an eye on you," Ariana said with a wink. She'd bounced back to her usual self, and hopefully, it would be enough to get her to talk to him over dinner. That was the other reason he proposed the Italian restaurant, you couldn't eat Italian food without wine.

He'd noticed her wine collection when she'd invited him in to pick up his plant. It was impressive, and if luck was on his side, it meant she wouldn't turn down a glass or two with him.

While he waited, he called the restaurant to reserve a table and then chatted with Mr. Darcy. "You need to keep watch over your momma. She's got some bad people after her." The dog stared at him like he understood every word, and John sure hoped he did.

"Okay, I'm ready."

Turning around at the sound of her voice, John was taken by surprise. He was used to seeing her in jeans and t-shirts or work out clothing. The dress was wow, just wow. It hugged her in all the right places and showed her lovely curves. Damn.

"You look amazing."

"Thank you, I wanted to look as good as you

do. After all, it's not every day I get to go to dinner with a sexy Navy SEAL." She was flirting with him unless he was so out of practice that he was imagining it. Maybe it was stress from everything she'd been through, no matter what had triggered it he didn't want it to stop.

CHAPTER 4

Flirting with John was dangerous considering her feelings for him. It was like looking down the loaded barrel of a gun and hoping no one pulled the trigger. He must think she lost her mind. Then again, he didn't look upset, more surprised and intrigued. That wasn't such a bad thing, was it?

Going out with John or anyone wasn't the best idea right now, but the look in his eyes when he'd asked her to dinner was irresistible. Putty in his hands or maybe Silly Putty. Thank God he didn't realize it. Being out with him put him in danger. Paul's accomplices made it perfectly clear they knew where and what she was doing all the time. The last thing she wanted was to put anyone in jeopardy. It was a good bet that Agent Rogers wouldn't be too thrilled either. Eh, he'd get over it. It's not the first time she'd ignored his advice.

"Are you sure you don't mind bringing Mr. Darcy?"

"Not at all. We had a chat and came to an understanding. No stinking up the place while we're eating." He said it with a completely straight face, and she burst out laughing.

"Oh yeah. He agreed to that?"

"He sure did. Right, buddy?" The dog sort of nodded his head and wagged his fluffy tail like he'd understood John's question.

Still giggling, she grabbed her purse from the table and turned to her dinner companions. "I'm ready if you are." She'd swear her dog was smiling as wide as her "date." For a brief moment, Ari wondered if Shira had somehow set this up with John. It would be just like her to butt into her love life. Then she stifled her snort. What love life?

John had Mr. Darcy's leash and held out his hand for her keys. After locking the door, he handed them back and took her hand.

"Can I ask you a question? I'm warning you though, it might piss you off."

John grinned, before he answered, "Sure. But I don't think you can piss me off. I'm pretty easy."

Easy, huh? She'd leave that comment alone for now. Especially since as he'd said it, he waggled his eyebrows. "Why didn't you call one of your women to have dinner with you? We haven't had a 'go to dinner' type of relationship."

If she hadn't been watching him closely, she would have missed the quick look of surprise before the slight smile returned. Curious.

"I was hungry, I like you. After spending the last few weeks with the guys, I thought it would be nice to have dinner with the fairer sex. And believe it or not, I don't have any women on speed dial. Is that okay with you?"

"Yes, of course. I just wondered about it, and why today? But I guess you answered that already."

"Exactly. I didn't have any food in my apartment, and I didn't want fast food. Eating alone wasn't all that appealing either. But does it matter?"

It didn't. Ari didn't like eating alone either. Mr. Darcy kept her from being as lonely even if he couldn't carry on a discussion. "Well, then. I'm glad you asked me."

"Me too." He was so laid-back and sweet it was easy to forget he was a trained killer. What would he think of Paul and all the danger he'd put her in. It would be nice to be able to confide in someone but with all the trouble surrounding her, she didn't want to bring anyone else into the mess.

As they walked down the street toward Amici's, she wondered if they were being watched. Would she get back home and find another email but this time it would be John's face with the red "x" over it? This constant worry about everything was driving her crazy.

Maybe it was time to let someone else in, someone who could help keep her safe. John was certainly qualified, but how would he feel about her when he found out the mess she was in? His protective tendencies would probably get a lot worse. Dealing with Colin was bad enough. There were so damn many rules she had to follow and they still hadn't caught anyone besides Paul. Fending off two overprotective males would be overwhelming.

"Ariana?"

"Hmm?"

"Where did you go?"

"What do you mean? I didn't go anywhere. I'm right here."

"Physically, yes, but mentally you were far away. I don't think you've heard a word I've said."

"Oh." How would she get out of that one? It wasn't the first time she'd zoned out since all of this started happening, and each time she'd been mortified. It made her seem like a ditz since she couldn't explain it to anyone. No, not couldn't, more like wouldn't. The first mistake she'd made was getting involved with someone at work. What had her mother always told her? Don't shit where you eat—yup a lovely thought. Her mother had been a hard woman, cold, and unlovable. But you knew where you stood with her. If she wasn't gone, she'd have given Ari hell for getting into this mess.

"You're doing it again."

"I'm sorry. I have a lot on my mind."

"Do you want to talk about it? I'm a great listener."

"I appreciate the offer. But I really don't know you that well."

"That's why I invited you to dinner, so we can change that."

She couldn't resist his bright smile. Genuine. Sexy. It softened the lines of his face and crinkled the edges of his sparkling eyes. "Maybe, we'll see."

"The offer's out there. Now, I hope you're hungry because I heard this place is amazing."

"I've heard that too. Lots of the people I work with love it here."

"I called ahead for a table while you were getting ready. I wanted to make sure we could get one outside since we have Mr. Darcy."

"Thank you. I should have thought about that."

"No worries, I've got your six."

"Six? Oh, right." She couldn't have held back her smile if her life depended on it. He really was a wonderful guy. Why couldn't she have met him before Paul? How different life might have been? Then again, he probably wasn't the type to settle down either. She needed to remember that because the last thing she needed was to get attached to the wrong man again.

Handing her Mr. Darcy's leash, John went to check in with the hostess. While they waited, she looked around, taking note of the people and cars. At least she had Mr. Darcy at her side like he was on protection detail. It was cute and several of the diners smiled when they looked at them.

Nothing looked out of the ordinary that she could tell. But it wasn't her job, it was the agent parked in the car across the street. Colin told her about them but not their names. It was weird, and so she named them all Shadow and added a number. Tonight's detail, Shadow Four, looked the least friendly of all of them.

"We had perfect timing. Our table is ready."

Still holding Mr. Darcy's leash, she followed John and the hostess across the patio. She led them to a table tucked against the far wall. It looked very romantic. The best part was that both chairs were set against the wall so they could look out and neither of them would have their back to the street.

"Perfect, thank you. Mr. Darcy won't be in anyone's way here."

"It's what I was thinking too," John said with a wide grin. Then he pulled out a chair and waited for her to sit down. She couldn't remember the last time a man held a chair for her. In fact, she didn't think it had ever happened. If she ever met his mother, she'd have to thank her for his manners.

"Thank you."

"You're welcome. C'mere, Mr. Darcy. Have a seat next to me." Ari couldn't believe how well he listened to John. It almost made her jealous —almost.

"Mr. Darcy seems to really like you."

"I like him too. How did you meet him?"

"At the shelter. I started helping out on weekends. One weekend when I went in, he was there cowering in his cage. Someone found him lying by the highway and thought he was dead. They brought him to the shelter and the poor guy was starving and covered with fleas and ticks."

"Wow, poor guy."

"Right away I knew I had to bring him home with me. But he had a lot of healing to do first. They were also worried he wouldn't ever be a good house pet because of all he'd probably been through. That it would take a while for him to let me touch him. But they were wrong."

"How did you win him over?"

"I climbed into one of the large cages with him and offered him treats. After a couple of hours, he was eating out of my hand."

"He's lucky to have you."

"No, I'm lucky to have him."

They had a connection, unlike anything she'd ever had with a dog. She swore he knew what was in her heart and soul.

The hostess handed them menus. "Your server will be over in just a bit to take your drink orders. If you need anything, just let any of the staff know. Enjoy your meal." If the food was as good as she'd heard, Ari had no doubt they would. The menu had just about every Italian dish she'd ever heard of and trying to narrow it down to one thing was a lot more difficult than she expected.

"Order whatever you like, this one's on me. It's the least I can do since you've been taking such good care of my plant, errr, Miss Jade."

Ari giggled. It sounded funny when he said it. "You don't have to call her that just because I do."

"Well, I wouldn't want her to get confused and start dropping leaves."

"Now you're teasing me."

"Maybe a little. It's too easy. Seriously, though, I can't tell you how much I appreciate that you take care of her. It's the first plant I've owned that has lived longer than a month."

"Somehow that doesn't surprise me. How long have you had her?" It was an easy question, so what caused the shadow that slid across his face? Did the plant belong to an ex-girlfriend, someone he loved?

"Not too long, actually. I got it shortly after I moved in. But then I was recertified for duty and started going away a lot." Okay, so maybe not an old girlfriend. But something was bothering him.

"I'm sorry."

"For what?"

"I don't know. But I get the feeling you're upset." She'd surprised him, it was obvious from the expression on his face.

"Nope, everything is fine. I'm just not used

to people being able to read me. Actually, I meant that I'm not used to anyone other than my Team noticing my feelings. Nothing gets by them."

Before she could say anything else, their server appeared at the table. "Would you like something to drink? We don't have a full bar, but here's the wine list. We have a full selection of soft drinks, and Pellegrino if you'd prefer that over tap water."

John looked through the wine list. "Ariana, would you prefer red or white?"

"Get whatever you like better, I'm probably not going to have any."

"Why not? I know you enjoy wine, I've seen your collection. C'mon, have some wine. We aren't driving, and I'm sure Mr. Darcy will be able to get us home if we're a bit tipsy."

It was all Ari could do not to roll her eyes. "Fine, how about a pinot noir then. Unless you don't like reds?" How did he make her cave like that? One minute she's saying no, then she's picking the wine.

"I like both, and since I'm having lasagna, red is perfect." John chose a bottle and asked for a bottle of Pellegrino for the table, and an antipasto platter. She was impressed and a little surprised. This was a side of him she hadn't seen before.

"Did you decide on an entrée?"

"I think I'll have the lasagna, too. Although, I should get something different. But after you said lasagna, it made my decision for me."

"I'm sorry. It's been a long while since I've had it. When I think of Italian, lasagna is always the first thing that comes to mind and my mouth starts watering."

"It's okay, I can't remember the last time I had it either."

The wine arrived, and the server poured just enough in their glasses for them to sample the flavor. When John approved she filled their glasses halfway and left the bottle on the table. Shortly after that, she brought the tray of antipasto.

"Shall we toast?"

"Sure. Do you have something in mind?"

"How about my sexy dinner partner and his owner."

It was the last thing Ari expected and burst into laughter before she could stop herself. The couples at the other tables turned to stare at them, which made her laugh harder. John somehow managed to bring out a side of her she'd buried long ago. One she thought would never return.

"Oh yeah, I'll drink to that," she said after calming down. "Cheers."

"Thank you again for coming with me."

"And thank you for asking and twisting my arm."

"I didn't twist it, did I? Okay, but I didn't have to do it too hard."

"No, you were just a little pushy."

He tried to look contrite but didn't come close to pulling it off. But she didn't care, she was lost in his eyes. They were the deepest green she'd ever seen, like looking into a pair of glittering emeralds. The fine lines at their corners and the thin scar on the right side of his face didn't take away from his looks at all. He was perfect imperfection, it wouldn't make sense to anyone else, but it did to her. She'd often wondered about the scar since she'd met him, but asking wouldn't be polite. Some things her mother had ingrained in her so well she still could hear the woman's sharp voice.

He smiled and touched their wine glasses

together in another silent toast. She'd love to know what he was thinking, but she didn't want to break the spell. Her heart was doing somersaults in her chest, and the moment seemed so intimate she almost reached out and traced the scar with her finger.

Mr. Darcy chose that moment to woof, and the spell was broken. Focusing on swirling the wine in her glass, she settled herself back down. The heat in her cheeks probably gave her away.

"What's up, buddy?" John asked her fluffy companion, the mood breaker, and farting king of the world.

"Woof."

"Do you want some bread?"

"Woof." And making sure John got the point, he put his paw on his leg.

"Mr. Darcy, stop that."

"Don't worry. It's fine. Can I give him bread or do you think it will aggravate his ummm issue?" He whispered the last. Probably a good idea. The last thing they needed was the other customers knowing it was Mr. Darcy if he accidentally let a few stinkers loose.

"Bread shouldn't bother him. I wouldn't give him too much, no sense taking chances."

"I agree. I'd rather not be banned for life."

"No kidding." He held out a piece of bread to her four legged-fuzzball, but he turned his head away. "What's wrong? I thought you wanted it?"

"Woof." Again, he put his paw on John's leg and looked at the table.

"You want me to put butter on it?"

"Woof."

"What kind of a dog are you raising here?"

She had no idea, it was a first. Usually, he was thrilled to take whatever she offered. What strange weirdness was this? Sure enough, after John buttered the bread he took it and laid down under the table.

"I've never seen him do that before."

"Obviously, he watched us put butter our bread and decided he wanted the same thing." A low woof came from under the table in acknowledgment. Her dog was definitely one of a kind.

John refilled their wine glasses. "If you keep this up I'm going to be too buzzed to eat."

"From two glasses?"

"I didn't eat a lot today. Actually, I think I only had a couple of the cookies Shira brought over. Things got a little crazy and I was too distracted to eat."

"I'm sorry to hear that. The offer still stands, I'm a great listener if you want to talk about it."

"Thanks, I really do appreciate your offer. We just don't know each other that well."

"Hopefully, this dinner will help change that. I really like you, a lot more than like. I'm hoping we can see where this can lead."

He'd rendered her speechless. Up until he'd invited her to dinner she figured she was just a plant sitter to him. "I don't know what to say." To say she was surprised was the understatement of the year.

"You don't have to say anything. I wanted to lay my cards on the table. I haven't been around another woman I wanted to see more than once in years. I am hoping we can see where this leads."

"A poker analogy?"

"Yeah, well I did just get back from three months with a bunch of men."

Ari took a sip of wine. He was so easy to be around. It was kind of scary. Her judge of character hadn't been the best, what if he turned out to be worse than Paul? John must have seen her indecision because he didn't wait for her to answer.

"I have an idea. How about we play twenty questions? You can ask me anything and unless it's classified I'll answer. What do you say?"

Did she want to go down that road? There were too many things she'd rather not share. But then he didn't know about the asshat and his accomplices. Her secrets should be safe. "Sure, but I reserve the right to not answer."

"That's not fair."

"I don't have classified stuff, and I won't know if you're lying or not to avoid answering."

"Lie? No way. I'm a SEAL, remember?" Again, she'd swear a shadow passed across his face.

"Fine, but I reserve the right to say no to one question. Okay?"

"Yup, that works. You go first," he said before picking up a piece of salami and taking a bite.

Before she could ask her first question, the server brought their meals. As Ari cut into her lasagna and the aroma of fresh basil and oregano teased her senses, she decided the questions could wait. "I need to try this first."

John nodded, already digging in. Obviously, he wasn't all about savoring the experience.

"It's really good. I'm glad you dragged me here."

John chuckled. "Me too. I thought for sure you were going to turn me down. I'm so glad you didn't."

"Eating alone gets old after a while."

"Exactly. Although MREs in the jungle with a bunch of dudes isn't my idea of a nice meal."

Ari could picture it. His team in camo, grabbing food where they could while dealing with bad guys.

Not even through half the slice of lasagna, and Ari was already stuffed. While they were eating, Mr. Darcy remained under the table. He was extremely well behaved, just as John promised. There hadn't been any gaseous outbursts at all. She couldn't wait to share that piece of news with Shira. To reward his good behavior, she slipped him a few breadsticks. He gobbled them right up and didn't demand butter.

Taking another sip of wine, she contemplated what she wanted to ask. "Are you ready for your first question?"

"Sure am," John answered as he refilled their wine glasses.

A warm, satisfying feeling washed over her while they were eating. She was more relaxed than she'd been in ages. It was John, all John. It didn't hurt that it was like living a dream— dinner with the leading man of more than one late-night fantasy.

"I can ask anything, right?"

"Yup. Go for it."

"Why did you decide to become a SEAL?"

He took a swallow of wine before answering, and she had to control the desire to squirm in her chair. Maybe it was too personal to start with. But then it was better than the one she wanted to ask, 'how did you get your scar?'

"It was a no-brainer really. My father was a SEAL. I grew up idolizing him. I told everyone who asked that I was going to be a SEAL when I grew up, just like my father."

"Wow, I can't even imagine knowing what you wanted to be when you were so young. I must have changed my mind fifty million times." Just the thought of all of her 'plans' made her smile.

"I won't say it was easy, but my dad made it

seem that way. Since I had my plan all ready, I enlisted through the SEAL Challenge Contract. Basically, it's a Seaman to SEAL program. By doing that I was guaranteed a chance to become a SEAL candidate. After that, the fun happened. There were a lot of steps to go through. But it was all worth it."

"I didn't realize you couldn't just join as a SEAL."

"Nope. But don't feel bad, most people don't realize that."

"Your father must be so proud of you."

"I like to think so. We lost him before I graduated from BUD/S."

"Oh no. I'm so sorry."

"It was a long time ago." He covered her hand with his and gave it a gentle squeeze. His touch startled her and she fought the urge to pull her hand away. "Are you okay?"

"Yeah," she answered, hoping he couldn't hear the too-fast beating of her heart from his touch. "That was more than one question though."

"It's okay." He poured more wine in her glass. When had she finished the last one? "My turn. What do you do for a living? I know you can't be a full-time plant sitter."

Relieved it was a 'safe' question, she took a sip of the Pellegrino water this time, determined not to get any tipsier. "I work in technology for a Naval contractor on base. But that's all I can tell you."

"Or you'll have to kill me?"

"Yeah, kind of like that." She softened her words with a wide grin. His answering smile went all the to his eyes and she'd swear they twinkled. Too sexy for his own good, that's for sure.

"Thank you," John said, still grinning.

"Huh?" What could he be thanking her for?

"You said I was sexy."

"Shit, I said that out loud? Oh my God, no more wine for me."

"I confessed earlier that I'm attracted to you. I'm happy to know the feeling is mutual."

It seemed sudden. They'd had casual interactions for months but that's it. Naturally suspicious, after all the shit Paul put her through, her instincts raised goosebumps on her arms. It didn't add up. Was he really interested in her? Or was something else behind all of this?

"I guess I just don't understand why the sudden change. Our interactions have been just neighborly. Nothing more. Then tonight you tell me you're attracted to me. What changed? And for the record, I don't do one night stands."

When he didn't answer at first, her stomach knotted and her mouth could have passed for the Sahara Desert. Grabbing the glass of water like it was a lifeline, she downed it.

As soon as she put the empty glass back on the table, he refilled it. His gentle smile went a long way to calming her frayed nerves. It had to be the wine. Normally, she wasn't this unsettled. Shira would be surprised to see her like this. Calm under pressure was her mantra or one of them no matter how much shit hit the fan. So why was flirting with John affecting her so much? Maybe it was because of the email she'd gotten earlier.

The last thing she expected was for him to burst into laughter. He tried to muffle it behind his hand after a few of the couples at the other tables closest turned around.

CHAPTER 5

Every moment they spent together pulled him further under her spell. No matter how hard he tried to focus on her safety, all she had to do was smile and he was lost. How he'd managed to get through the meal without having to excuse himself to rearrange, he had no idea. It took all of his will not put her onto his lap and kiss her until neither of them could breathe. And the desire didn't stop there. They barely knew each other, yet he couldn't imagine not having her in his life. She was perfect, or as Elwood liked to say, 'the whole enchilada'.

Inside her short, curvy, body was a heart of gold and a sense of humor and a stubborn streak a mile wide. But losing control would put her in danger. The FBI had her under surveillance. It would have been impossible to miss the black car sitting across the street from the restaurant even if he hadn't known they were watching. He'd bet anyone that whoever sent her the email earlier also had their eyes on her. If he didn't find a way to make her open up to him, he'd have a hell of a time keeping her safe. Yeah, Colin wanted him to back off once he was cleared hot and joined Charlie Team, but he couldn't have walked away even if he wasn't falling for her.

Still chuckling about the one-night stand remark, then the slight flush on her cheeks and look of confusion sank into his thick brain. Was she serious? Why the hell would she think that's what he wanted? Sure, she'd mentioned his "other women," but she must not have been paying attention. There hadn't been a woman in his apartment or bed in over two months.

"I'm sorry, Baby. I didn't mean to laugh. But that was the last thing I expected to hear you say."

"Baby? I don't think we're quite to that point, are we? It's only our first dinner. And why was that so surprising? Don't you think I'm attractive enough?" Ari's voice wobbled, close to tears or possibly anger, he wasn't sure.

"Dammit, Ari. That couldn't be further from the truth. I've been sitting here for the last hour wondering how you'd taste, what you'd feel like in my arms, and in my bed. So don't for one minute even think that."

Her mouth opened and then closed without saying a word. Her cheeks had turned a bright pink and her eyes were wide with surprise. Those blue-green eyes, sweet baby Jesus, it was like swimming in the waters of the Caribbean. But continuing down this path was dangerous for them. As much as he loved teasing her it was torture on his body. He needed to focus. Swearing under his breath, he chastised himself. He needed to rein it in if he was going to get her into a safe house.

"You say all that and then wonder why I think that's what you want?"

"There is no way one night would ever be enough. A thousand nights won't quench my thirst for you."

He watched his words permeate her tipsy brain and turned an even darker shade of pink.

This dinner was not about seduction, it was supposed to be about ensuring her safety. Even if he was relieved that his feelings were finally out in the open. Now wasn't the time or place to explain he was serious and that one night would never be enough for him. He had no doubt that once he had her, he'd never be able to let her go.

"I think you might have had too much wine."

"Nope, I'm fine. The first day I saw you at the gym I knew you were special. You were so serious, so determined to get it right and do it all by yourself. I was worried you'd get hurt."

"I didn't have a clue what I was doing. I just wanted to get stronger. To be able to protect myself…"

There, the opening he'd been waiting for. "Protect yourself? Wouldn't a self-defense class be better?"

"Not really. Maybe."

"What's going on, Ariana?"

"Nothing. Don't worry. I've got it covered."

"I'm not buying that. You said you had to protect yourself. From who?"

"I knew you would go all Neanderthal on me."

"What?"

"You know, troglodytic? Like a caveman and I don't mean the ones in the GEICO commercial."

John chuckled and shook his head. "You think I'm a caveman?"

"Yup. Look how overbearing you've been about the door."

"It's for your safety."

"And why were you worried about it? It's why I keep things to myself. If you found out about the trouble I'm in you'd probably lose your mind."

"You can't say stuff like that and then not tell me. What kind of trouble?" He hated lying and manipulating her, but it was the only way. It's how he'd planned for this to work, so why did it feel so shitty?

"I shouldn't have had that last glass of wine. Damn. Two glasses don't usually get to me especially when I'm eating." He didn't have the heart to tell her she'd had three or maybe close to four. He'd kept her glass-topped off and barely touched his. It made him an asshole, but she was so stubborn. If he could have come up with another way to get her to let down her guard he'd have done it.

"Tell me about this trouble."

"Are you finished?" The server interrupted.

"Yes, thank you. It was absolutely delicious," Ari said with a smile.

"Would you like me to pack up the rest to bring home?"

"Sure, that would be great. Thank you."

"Can I bring anything else? Dessert? Our tiramisu is outstanding, but we also have gelato and cheesecake."

"I couldn't eat anything else."

"Do you want to get something to go? We can have it with coffee when we get home." He wasn't ready to let her slip through his hands. He was a man on a mission, and he always finished what he started. At first, he thought she would say no, but she smirked as she met his eyes.

"Okay, fine. Do you want to share a tiramisu?"

"Sounds perfect. Could you pack one for us with her leftovers?"

"Of course. I'll be back with that and your check."

"Ariana, just because we were interrupted doesn't mean I'll forget."

"I didn't think you would. Isn't that the reason for dessert?"

"Partly, the other part is I really love tiramisu. I've had it all over the world so I couldn't pass it up."

"Really? You've traveled that much?"

"Yes, and I'll be happy to tell you all about it if you want. But now I want to hear about the trouble you're in. It's why you were crying earlier, right?"

"Yes, but it's a long story. A boring, screwed up, dangerous story."

"I like those," John said with a smile.

The server was back. "Here you go. I hope you enjoyed your meal and that you'll come back again."

"It was excellent. We'll definitely be back." Ariana raised her eyebrows as he responded, but when she didn't contradict him he was more relieved than he should have been. He gave the server cash for the bill. It was more expensive than his usual dinners, but as far as he was concerned the time with Ariana was priceless.

"Mr. Darcy, are you awake down there?" Ari

asked and a fluffy tan head popped up from under the tablecloth with a woof.

"Are you ready, Baby?"

"Yes. Thank you for dinner. It was delicious, but I don't understand why you're calling me baby all of a sudden."

"I'm sorry. I've been calling you that in my head for months. If it really bothers you I'll try to stop, but I can't promise I won't slip."

She looked at him and seemed to consider what he'd said. He held his breath waiting to find out if she'd shoot him down or take a chance. "Honestly, I'm not sure. It's weird but I don't hate it."

"I'll try to use it sparingly until you like it. Will that work?" he asked with a gentle smile and was rewarded with one of hers.

"Yeah, I think I can live with that. It really was nice getting out of the apartment."

"Our evening isn't over yet. Don't even think about ditching me at your door."

She laughed as she grabbed the bag with her leftovers and got up from the table. "I didn't think it would work."

"You thought right. There's no putting anything over on you."

"I'm not so sure about that," she replied as her grin melted away.

Not sure what stole her smile, he put his hand on the small of her back and guided her through the maze of tables and onto the sidewalk with Mr. Darcy staying by his side.

"What are you thinking about?"

"You, the situation, everything. I'm worried if you find out you'll get hurt or I will."

"Don't be. Let's be serious for a moment. Whether or not you believe me, I will never intentionally hurt you."

"How can you know that?"

"Because I do. You don't know me that well, but I'm hoping to rectify that. You're amazing and I enjoy your company." Having this discussion in the middle of the sidewalk was not ideal. John needed to get her out of the open, it was too dangerous. Taking her hand, they headed back to the apartment complex. The car with the FBI agents followed.

"You only think I'm amazing. If you knew everything you wouldn't think so anymore."

"Then tell me. I promise you that I'm not going anywhere. Even if you're not interested in going any further, I'm your friend."

She'd stopped and stared up at him. The sun had set while they were eating, and the moon bathed her skin in a soft glow. She looked angelic and took his breath away. God help him once he held her in his arms and tasted her.

"I'd like to believe you, John. But my track record hasn't been great."

"You'll never know if you don't take a chance." As they walked along, his head was on swivel checking their six. He wanted to trust that if someone attempted to hurt her that the FBI agent would handle the situation.

"That's true. If I tell you, you have to promise me one thing."

"What's that?"

"That you won't go apeshit and be a Neanderthal man."

"Without knowing what you're going to tell me it's hard to make that promise. I'm a SEAL my first instinct is to protect. Can I promise to try my best?"

"I guess that'll have to do. But if you go crazy I'll sic Mr. Darcy on you. Trust me, he can be ferocious when he needs to be. Right, Mr. Darcy?"

On cue, the fluffy furball woofed making them laugh.

"You really adopted a great dog. I'm glad you found each other."

"Me too. I can't believe he's only been with me for a month."

"That means it's a good thing. My mom always said that if time flew by you were happy, it only drags when you're miserable."

"I've never heard that before, but it makes a lot of sense. Does your mom live close?"

"Nope, she lives in Virginia with my sister."

"You have a sister? I really don't know you at all."

"I told you that you can ask me anything."

By then they'd gotten back to their building. John pressed the numbers into the keypad and opened the door. "Do you want to go to my apartment or yours?"

She gave him a questioning look.

"Dessert, remember? And you promised you'd tell me what's going on with you."

"You really don't forget anything, do you?"

"Not much," he answered with a huge grin. She was pretending to be exasperated, but she couldn't hold back her smile.

"Mine will be easier, and Mr. Darcy can have his real dinner and some water."

They didn't have long to wait for the elevator and soon they were on their floor. Her apartment was closer, and her door was visible from the elevator.

"Shit. Get behind me and hold on to Mr. Darcy."

"Why, what's…"

"Shhh. Your door is wide open. I need you to stay out of sight and call nine-one-one. Mr. Darcy, stay and watch our girl."

"Okay."

He hated hearing the quiver in her voice, but it couldn't be helped. She wasn't alone, and he had no intention of letting anything happen to her. Of course, it was one of the few times he wasn't carrying. It was stupid on his part. Especially since he knew she was in danger.

Double-checking to make sure she was protected and listened to him about calling the police, he approached the door. The door jamb had a long crack and the knob was smashed. Whoever wanted to get in hadn't been kidding. Standing out of range of a gun, he pushed the door open with his foot. Silence. Opening the door wider, he waited again. When nothing happened, he peered around the smashed door frame then stepped inside.

Holy fuck. It looked nothing like the apartment he'd been in earlier that day. Every piece of furniture in the living room had been upended and the fabric shredded. The books pulled from their shelves and the cabinets in the kitchen hung open with dishes strewn across the floor.

They'd been searching for something and he wondered if they'd found it. He was glad they'd done this when she wasn't home. The thought of her being there when they broke through the door made his blood boil. God help them if they hurt a hair on her head. Maybe they were smart enough not to want an assault charge or worse on their heads.

Going from room to room he checked for intruders, but they were long gone leaving the apartment destroyed. It looked like a bomb had gone off. The sons-of-bitches would pay for this when he caught them, and he would catch them.

He wished there was a way to keep Ariana from seeing the devastation. Or at least a way to soften the blow. All he could do is promise that he'd get these guys so she could feel safe again. As soon as he got her settled either in the safe house or his apartment—he was opting for the second choice—he had a few phone calls of his own to make.

"Nine-one-one, what's your emergency?"

"My name is Ariana Nelson. My apartment was broken into."

"Are you in the apartment now? Are you in immediate danger? Are the intruders still there?"

"I don't think I'm in danger."

"What's your address?"

"Twenty-two eighty-nine Alameda Boulevard. Apartment seven-oh-three."

"A unit should be there within ten minutes. Are you alone? Do you want me to stay on the line with you?"

"No, I'm okay. I have a friend with me. He actually went into the apartment to check it out."

"Ma'am, tell him not to touch anything until the officers get there."

"I will, but I'm sure he already knows."

"Okay. Are you sure you don't want to stay on the call until the officers get there?"

"Thank you, but I'm fine."

Ari disconnected the phone and looked down at Mr. Darcy who was sitting obediently at her side. John hadn't come back, but she couldn't hear anything from the apartment either. Whoever had broken in was probably long gone.

"C'mon, Mr. Darcy, let's see how bad it is."

"Woof." He didn't budge, hadn't even stood up.

"Come, Mr. Darcy. Don't make me pull you."

"Woof." Still, he didn't move.

"What's wrong with you? Fitzwilliam Darcy, you need to listen to me." But instead of getting up he looked from her to the apartment door and back to her again. It was as if he was saying, John told us to stay so we're staying. "Whose dog are you? You're supposed to listen to me."

"He's protecting you. I told you to stay put

for your protection. I'm glad the dog listened at least."

"I didn't go in."

"Nope you didn't, but only because he wouldn't get up."

Dammit, she was busted. Not only was he a Neanderthal but he had ears that could hear a fart a mile away.

"Whatever it is you're thinking, you have an evil expression, and it's kind of creepy."

"Really?" She growled, and even Mr. Darcy looked at her. "You promised not to go all caveman on me, remember?"

"I promised I'd try. I didn't count on this."

"Ugh. It's not your problem."

"It is now. What did the police say?"

"They'd be here in ten minutes or so."

Ari had no sooner said it when Mr. Darcy began howling a sure sign the police weren't far away. He was practically a professional and had great range. The first time he'd done it, she'd wondered if at some point he'd belonged to a Fire Department, but she couldn't imagine they'd have let him run away.

"We should probably go downstairs and let them in," John said as the elevator doors opened revealing Shadow Four with two police officers. "Who's with the police?"

"My protection detail."

"Your what?"

"Protection. He's an FBI agent. He's one of four men who are stuck following me around. I call them all Shadow because I don't know their names. This is part of what I was going to tell you."

"I see. I'm surprised they only have one on you at a time. There should have been someone guarding your place."

"Nope, they only follow me."

"Miss Nelson, please stay in the hallway while we clear the apartment," Shadow Four said in his most authoritative voice. Shadow One and Two weren't so bad, but Three and Four were totally over the top.

"The Crime Scene Unit is on the way. In the meantime, can you tell us what happened?"

"Of course, but it's not much. We just got back from dinner…"

"We?"

"Yes, my friend and I were at dinner. That's him talking to the FBI agent. His name is John Dillon, he's in the Navy. If you need more information than that, he can give it to you."

"Got it. How long were you and your boyfriend gone?"

"A couple of hours, but he's not my boyfriend."

"Yes, I am," John said as he appeared at her side.

The policeman looked back and forth between them and shrugged. It was obvious he'd heard the argument before.

"Okay, so you were at dinner for a couple of hours and then came back when?"

"Just before I called, so whatever time the nine-one-one call came in. We'd just stepped off the elevator when John saw the door smashed in."

"Did either of you see anyone?"

"No."

"Did you go into the apartment?"

"I didn't. I stayed out here with my dog to call you."

"I went in to make sure no one was around, but I didn't touch anything. I know how to deal with crime scenes."

The officer nodded and kept making notes.

Ari wanted to see her apartment. From John's actions, it couldn't be good. They probably wouldn't let her stay there now. Where would she go? She had no idea which hotels allowed dogs. Damn, that made her think of Colin. She probably should have called him right after the police. Hopefully, Shadow Four took care of that.

CHAPTER 6

Abing sounded just before the elevator doors slid open. John pushed Ari behind him, and both officers drew their guns. All the commotion probably took about five years off of Mrs. Laramie's life. Ari felt horrible for the elderly woman and was glad she didn't need medical attention.

"What's going on? Ari, John?"

"I'm sorry, Mrs. Laramie. Someone broke into Ari's apartment, so we are a little jumpy."

"I'll say," the feisty octogenarian replied. "I almost peed my pants. Thank goodness for Depends." It shouldn't have been that funny, but Ari started giggling which turned into full-blown laughter. She tried to stop. She really did.

Everyone probably thought she'd lost her mind, but Mrs. Laramie smiled and winked.

"Did you happen to see anyone hanging around that you didn't recognize?" One of the officers asked as she headed down the hallway to her apartment.

"Actually, there were a few Asian gentlemen in the lobby earlier. They had a couple of boxes with them and I thought they were moving in."

"Do you think you could give a description to a sketch artist?"

"I'm not sure, my eyesight isn't what it was. But if it will help Ari, I'll be happy to try."

The doors slid open again, and it was a repeat of the last time. Ari swore she was going to have bruises from John pushing her around. She knew he was in full-blown protection mode, but it was getting out of hand. From the stink that wafted around her, even Mr. Darcy wasn't taking it well.

"Stop right there," one of the police officers demanded.

"That won't be necessary."

Ari couldn't see who'd arrived on the scene because John's wide shoulders were blocking her view, but she recognized that voice—Special

Agent Colin Rogers. The shit was going to hit the fan now.

"Wait just a minute," the older of the two officers held out his hand. "You need to stop right there."

Ari peeked around John and saw the pinched expression on Colin's face. Yup, he was super pissed off. At least this time it wasn't her fault, right? Wait, it couldn't be her fault, could it?

Colin flashed his badge to the officers. "I'm Special Agent Colin Rogers of the FBI. We'll be taking over now. But thank you for the quick response."

"I don't know..." the other officer started to object.

"Call your captain, he'll tell you. Oh and Mrs. Laramie, you won't need to worry about the sketch artist. Thank you for offering."

The officers didn't look very happy about being dismissed, but after a call to their captain, they nodded at Colin and left the crime scene to the FBI.

The short, silver-haired woman looked him over and nodded. "If you need anything, child, let me know."

"Thank you, Mrs. Laramie. Have a good evening." It was the oddest thing to be happening in the middle of a crime scene, one more item to add to her list of experiences she'd never hoped to have.

"John Dillon? What are you doing here?"

"I live here, but it's nice to see you too." Ari was confused. Did they know each other? And why did Colin look like he swallowed a porcupine? She wished she was better at reading people. Duh, if she had been she wouldn't be in this mess.

"You two know each other?" she asked as she stepped around John. There was no way she was in danger with all the testosterone around her. It was more likely they'd shoot each other. Men.

"Yes," they answered in unison and exchanged glances. This was getting weirder by the minute.

"We met in college and were roommates," John said.

"Wow. That's a crazy coincidence to run into each other now."

"Yes, it is. We'll have to get together soon

and catch up," Colin answered. "But for now, I need to move Ms. Nelson to a safe house."

"No. I told you earlier, I'm staying here."

"But Ari it's not safe," Colin said exasperation coloring his words.

They were going to double-team her now? They could try, but she had other ideas.

"The apartment is trashed. All the furniture is ruined. You can't stay there. Besides, the door is broken, and we can't get it fixed tonight," John said.

"I want to see it."

"I don't think that's a good idea."

Ari leveled a look at John that had been known to stop lesser men in their tracks. But it didn't seem to bother him one bit.

"Don't. Just stop. What did I tell you about being a Neanderthal around me?

"But..." She turned in time to see Colin trying to cover the smile on his face. Like she was any happier with him.

"I'm going in unless there's some other reason I can't?" She directed the question to Colin.

"If you promise not to touch anything I'll take you through it. I want to take a look."

John started to object, but Colin gave him a sharp look and stopped whatever he was going to say. She was ready to tell them to all get lost, it was her apartment, she was a grown woman.

"Can you hold onto Mr. Darcy?"

"Of course."

"You stay here with John. He'll take care of you. Be a good boy." Mr. Darcy didn't look very happy about her leaving him and let out a low growl, but she knew Colin wouldn't want the dog muddying up his crime scene. "It's okay. I promise I'll be right back," Ari said as she handed the leash to John.

"Baby, you have to remember it's just stuff. It can all be replaced. Right?"

"Okay." She caught Colin's raised eyebrow at the endearment but it was the last thing she wanted to deal with. The apartment was her main focus, she wasn't even sure if she could stay there tonight or anytime soon. But she needed to see it, then she'd figure out her next steps.

Colin went in first, and after what John had said she tried to prepare herself for the worst. But there was no way in hell she could have been ready for the disaster that used to be her home. A loud gasp escaped as she gazed at the total destruction.

"Why would someone do this? I don't understand. I don't have anything valuable."

"Unfortunately it's how the world is. You're a good person and haven't been exposed to this type of thing. And if I had to guess, I'd say these are the same people who sent that email earlier. It's all part of trying to keep you from testifying."

"But you don't know for sure."

"No, not yet. But if it is them, they won't stop until they get what they want."

"And they thought destroying my home would do that?"

"With the trial approaching, they're probably getting desperate. It's going to continue to escalate. I wish you'd reconsider Witness Protection."

"We've been over this, and unless you can tell me my life is in danger and by whom, I'm not going into WITSEC. I told you that before. I don't want to give up my life, my friends, my job."

"I understand, but is it more important than

staying alive? I'm not sure you'll be safe after the trial."

"We're working on it. But it would make sense that it's the people Chen worked with. He was low down in the chain but can identify all of them and they probably think you can too. If they want to hurt you, they won't stop until they succeed."

"I don't know anything. Paul never involved me in any of it."

"But they don't know that, and until we can connect the dots you need to be in a safe house. I think they were looking for something. There's just too much destruction for it to be anything else."

"I don't have anything of value to anyone but me."

"Are you sure Paul didn't give you some-thing? A flash drive, a memory card? Anything like that?"

"No, I already told you. He didn't give me anything."

Colin was right about one thing. She couldn't stay there. Everything was trashed. But she'd be damned if she was going to let him put her in a safe house. She wished she could go to

Shira's, but that would put her in even more danger.

"Can I pack a small bag, toiletries, some clothing? I know I can't stay here. I'll get a hotel room."

"No..." This time the reply was in stereo. She turned around and John stood in the doorway with Mr. Darcy.

"I don't know what you were going to say, Colin, but no way. Besides, most of them won't let her bring a dog. I think she should stay with me. I have a spare bedroom."

"I would prefer she come with us to the safe house."

"Really? I think I can do a better job of protecting her. Your guys couldn't stop this. What makes you think you can stop what's coming next?"

"Because it's what we do. Protect our witnesses. Agent Charles was following his orders and watching the witness." Ahh, so Shadow Four's name was Agent Charles. She liked calling him Shadow Four better. The agent in question was talking into his earpiece and looked mighty uncomfortable.

"Still, it doesn't look like you've got a good handle on this."

"You have no idea what is in play here."

"Then why don't you tell me?"

"Excuse me. You two are going back and forth like I can't make my own decisions. You both need to back off. The testosterone in here is oppressive."

"You can't." Again, with the stereo answers. Just how well did they know each other? They were too in sync to have not seen each other for years.

"Excuse me, sir, they have the video and are running it through facial recognition." Saved by the Shadow. At least he'd saved something that evening. Maybe she was being too hard on him. He'd been following orders and she hadn't been hurt.

"Good."

"That's why you don't need Mrs. Laramie to sit with the artist?"

"Exactly. We have several cameras on the property, inside and out."

"I didn't know that."

"Ariana, contrary to what you seem to believe, we take your safety very seriously." The look on his face left no doubt he believed every word he'd said. But she still wasn't satisfied.

Unhappy with the options they'd discussed in front of her, she didn't have much choice. She'd have to pick one of them. If she stayed with John she was close to home. Mr. Darcy would be comfortable, and she'd still be able to go to work. Not knowing where the safe house was located, work might not be an option. But there was one big drawback to staying with him, second bedroom or not. It had been hard enough not to fall into his arms when they were in public. How the hell would she be able to live in the same space with him without ending up in bed?

"If she stays with me, I'll make sure she's safe and her life won't have to be as disrupted."

"She won't be able to go to work or anywhere else. I don't want her out in public."

"I wish you would stop talking about me like I'm not standing here."

Going back and forth and weighing the pros and cons of the two choices, she decided on John. Hopefully, she wouldn't regret the decision. One thing was for certain—there would be way more than twenty questions in her future.

At least she had no doubt he'd keep her safe. She wasn't as confident about the Shadows.

"I've decided to stay in John's apartment. Mr. Darcy knows him. You already have the building under surveillance, so it makes the most sense."

"I don't like it," Colin said. From the expression on his face, you'd think she told him he was fired.

"Sorry, but it's my decision. I'm sticking to it unless you can prove to me with absolute certainty that it's too dangerous to stay here."

Colin looked at his phone before answering. "No, I can't tell you that. I know John's a SEAL, so he's more than capable of protecting you should something happen. But I believe you'd be better off at the safe house."

"I understand, but I think I'll feel safer with John." She'd bet he was smirking right now, but she didn't want to turn around to check. "The trial is in one week, right? I promise I'll be extra careful."

"Fine. But if anything else happens, we're moving you to one of our safe houses. For the next week you won't be going anywhere without John or one of the agents on your detail. No work, no coffee shops, you're to stay inside as much as possible until after the trial."

"What?"

"It's already been cleared with your boss."

"Jesus, do you guys hear yourselves? You can't just take over my life like this."

"We can, since you're our key witness, and we will if that's the only way to keep you safe," Colin answered with an expression that said he was done with the discussion.

"Whatever. I'm going to pack a bag." When Shadow four started to follow her, she stopped him. "Alone. There is no imminent threat. I will be fine." Ari was done too. Exhausted, stressed, and on the verge of tears. The relaxed warmth from the wine at dinner was long gone. What she wouldn't give to be on the beach sipping margaritas in the sunshine. Instead, she was on house arrest for the next week.

As bad as the living room and kitchen had been, her bedroom was ten times worse. Tears welled up in her eyes as she saw the smashed angel figurine her grandmother had given her when she was seven. It was one of her prized possessions and now it was in pieces, like her life. Nothing was left alone, even her bed had been turned upside down and shredded.

Wading through the mess, she grabbed an overnight bag from the floor of the closet and threw in as much as she could that wasn't destroyed. For once she was happy she was a trust fund baby because it would take more than she had in the bank to set the place back to normal. After her parent's death, she'd sworn not to use the money except for an absolute emergency. Most of her childhood they'd traveled for work and left her with her grandmother. She barely knew them and didn't want their money. But if this didn't qualify as an emergency, she didn't know what would. Not that it made her feel any better.

After packing what she could, she gazed around the room. It didn't look anything like the room she'd gotten ready in a few hours earlier. This really was a nightmare and she prayed that the end was in sight.

When she walked into the living room, John and Colin had their heads close together. John was stiff, his face set in stone and Colin was flailing his hands around like one of those inflatable arm guys. Debating whether she wanted to interrupt their discussion, she hesitated in the doorway. "What's going on now? You're like little kids fighting over a toy. Seriously."

Startled, they turned toward her with guilty expressions on their faces.

"Are you ready?" John asked.

"Yes, I am. But I want to know what you were arguing about. Something's going on. This is my life, remember? I have a right to know."

They exchanged glances and John shrugged his shoulders.

"Well?"

When Colin nodded at Shadow Four, he went into the hall and left them alone. "I wish you'd reconsider about going to the safe house. But since it's clear that you won't, you will need to listen to John."

"I already said I would."

"Remember you said that, because the first time you don't listen, or go out when it's not absolutely necessary, you'll be going to the safe house."

"And if I don't agree?"

"It will be the safe house for you now."

"You can't make me go."

"Actually, we can. You're a witness in a

federal espionage case, I can and will do what-ever it takes to protect you."

Recognizing a brick wall when she saw one, Ari gave in. What choice did she have? "Fine. I'll accept your rules. But after the trial, all bets are off."

"We'll see," Colin replied.

John was smirking again. Seeing them standing next to each other was like looking at a couple of cover models for GQ magazine. They were the same height and build, but that was where the similarity ended. John was dark while Colin was light, with blond hair and blue eyes. The two of them must have had women lined up at their door in college. If things were differ-ent, she might have been attracted to Colin. But he made her feel like she was one of those too stupid to live women in bad books for being taken in by Paul.

"Do you have everything you need, Baby?"

"Yes, except for Mr. Darcy's bowls and food." Out of the corner of her eye, she saw Colin's surprised expression at John's use of the endearment. Was it bad she was glad?

"I grabbed them while you were packing.

See?" he said as he held up the bag of dry food and a plastic bag with the dog bowls.

"Thanks. Are we done, Colin? Or do you still need me?"

"You can go. I know where you'll be if something comes up. Remember what you promised."

"I don't think John would let me forget even if I wanted to. But what happens to the rest of my stuff? How do you keep people out now that the door is broken?"

The first, truly genuine smile she'd ever seen from Colin totally lit up his face. Probably a good thing he didn't do it more often. He'd never get anyone to believe he was an FBI agent. He was just too pretty.

"We'll put up some wood until the door can be replaced. One of the agents on your detail will check on it every few hours too."

"When will I be able to get more stuff?"

"After it's cleared, I'll let you know."

"I hope it doesn't take too long."

It was obvious that Colin was tired of her questions and wanted to get back to work when he turned to John. "Take good care of her."

"I will, you don't have to worry."

It was odd to walk away and leave Colin and Shadow Four standing in the disaster that had been her home. It was even odder to follow John to his apartment, but she didn't have a lot of options. She could either stay with him or go to a safe house that was located God only knew where. Blaming the tears swimming in her eyes on Mr. Darcy's latest stink bomb, she hoped she'd made the right choice.

CHAPTER 7

I t wasn't how John hoped the evening would play out, but it accomplished what he and Colin had set out to do—get her out of her apartment and into protective custody. He'd been surprised when Colin agreed to let Ariana stay with him.

It hadn't been an easy sell, even though it was the option she'd chosen. First, he had to promise to allow her security detail to have final say over everything. It was Colin's job, John understood that, but this was the woman who'd stolen his heart and his mind. If anyone thought they could protect her better than they, they were sorely mistaken, and he'd be happy to set them straight.

Unlocking the door to his apartment, he stood to the side to allow Ari and Mr. Darcy to enter first. "Welcome to your home away from home. The floorplan is like yours except for the extra bedroom. Hopefully, it won't be too much of an adjustment."

"Except this place doesn't look like a war zone," she answered softly as she stopped in the middle of the living room. If he hadn't been listening closely, he wouldn't have heard her. He wished more than anything he could have spared her from seeing how they'd destroyed her belongings.

"After the trial is over, you'll be able to go back home and fix it up good as new." It sounded lame, but he wasn't sure what else to say.

"I'm not so sure about that. Colin doesn't think they'll ever stop coming after me." There were tears in her voice, and when she faced him, her eyes were filled with liquid sadness waiting to slip down her face.

Without thinking, he wrapped his arms around her and pulled her tight against him. Rubbing his hands up and down her back, he hoped it would soothe some of her distress.

Anger, fear, and frustration poured out of her in big sloppy sobs. A crying woman is a man's worst nightmare. Following his instincts, he held her tighter. The warm tears soaked his shirt and his heart hurt for her. All of his alpha tendencies kicked into full gear. He wanted to pick her up and hide her away somewhere she'd always be safe even if it was the last thing she wanted. Mr. Darcy seemed just as unhappy and whimpered as he leaned against Ariana.

"I promise it will be okay. I won't let anything happen to you."

"Don't make promises you can't keep. You don't even know everything. Besides, if a team of FBI agents can't protect me, what makes you think one Navy SEAL can?"

"Well, that's where you're wrong. I have to make a couple of calls to rally the troops but trust me, there will be troops, and you will be safe."

Blinking back the last of her tears, she took the tissue he offered, blew her nose and wiped her tears. Her cheeks were bright red from crying and she was chewing on her bottom lip. Rubbing his thumb along her bottom lip, he slid it from under her teeth before she drew blood.

Tilting her head up so he could look into her eyes, his heart melted at the pain reflected in hers. Words wouldn't fix this, so he did the only thing he hoped would distract her.

Lowering his head, he gave her a chance to say no but she didn't say anything. This wasn't his ideal first kiss but it was the only way he could show her how much he cared that she might believe. Their eyes were locked together as he had his first taste. Sliding his tongue between her parted lips, he sighed in pleasure. Soft, warm, and sweet. He knew he should pull away, but he couldn't get enough of her. Wanting more, pulled her against his hips, knowing she'd feel his desire.

He'd tried to be gentle, and not push her. But when her mouth opened and her tongue timidly traced his lips, he was lost. Ari tasted like a fine wine, mellow with a hint of sweetness. When she pulled away it was like a part of him was ripped away. How had he gotten so attached to her? He'd never fallen for a woman so completely Somehow she'd managed to break down every one of the walls he'd put in place.

"Umm, can you put me down, please?"

"What? Oh God, yes." He hadn't even realized he'd lifted her into his arms. She was so petite her feet dangled off the floor. "You really are short," he said as he released her.

"I'm not, I'm fun-sized. You are a giant."

Again, she'd surprised him. He'd expected her to be upset that he'd kissed her, especially since he hadn't asked. But he'd never be sorry for that kiss. His heart felt whole again, something he'd never expected to happen. "I hope the kiss didn't upset you."

"It was unexpected, but honestly, I've wanted to do that for months."

"You have?" Damn, how did he not realize that? He'd sent plenty of signals. Apparently, so had she and he'd been too blind notice.

"I know you're not the relationship type, and after the hell my ex-Paul put me through, is still putting me through, I have a hard time trusting people, even ones I already know. He just about destroyed me. So having a relationship was not happening."

"Baby, I don't know the whole story, but I will never hurt you, not intentionally. I promise."

"I want to believe you, but it's not going to be easy. I'm sure after this evening I'm probably in shock. So take what I'm about to say with a grain of salt, okay?"

"I'll try." Damn, she was adorable. All of her emotions were clearly visible on her face as she tried to come up with what she wanted to say. And all he could focus on were her kiss swollen lips.

"I can't trust my judgment when it comes to men. I thought Paul was amazing when we first met, and now he's in jail for espionage. I've been attracted to you since I saw you in the gym. I almost peed my pants when you came over to talk to me."

"Really? I'd never have guessed. You were so reserved."

"Oh man, you have no idea. But I'd decided that men were off-limits, especially Navy SEALs. I've heard all the rumors and seen it in action. We've watched them go home with a different woman almost every night."

"Don't convict all of us based on a few. It's true some of the guys are like that, but it's mostly we get back from a mission, especially if there were close calls. But I am not one of them. I haven't been out with a woman in months."

"Really?" she said then chewed on the

corner of her fingernail.

"Yup. I swear."

"I guess I'm not as observant as I thought. But…" Her eyes met his, and they were like crystal clear blue-green pools. "I, uhh, the kiss was amazing but I'm not good relationship material. You'd be better off with someone who doesn't have so much baggage."

Ari never looked more adorable than at that moment, and he couldn't hold back his chuckle. She was something else. He didn't care what she said after they got the dirtbag put away for life, he'd show her just how great she could be at relationships.

"How about we agree to disagree on that point. You've had a long, stressful day. I'd hoped this would go a little differently, but there's always tomorrow."

"That's for sure."

"How about you get settled into the spare room. I have a few phone calls to make. If you'd like we can have some wine, or coffee and the tiramisu. Or you can just get some rest."

"I'd completely forgotten about dessert. Dinner seems like days ago."

"I know, Baby. I almost forgot the bag, but I

caught Mr. Darcy sniffing at it. The last thing we needed to deal with tonight is tiramisu doggy farts."

"Oh, yeah, he's sneaky. Aren't you, Mr. Darcy?" The dog actually looked contrite. It was amazing how much he seemed to understand them. If he'd believed in that type of thing, he might even think there was a touch of magic afoot.

The gassy furball followed her into the bedroom and curled up at her feet, while John pulled out his cell texted Elwood and his old SEAL boss, Chase Brennan. After being medically retired, he'd opened up a security firm in Florida. The last time Chase was in Calfornia, he'd ended up saving Faith from a stalker and taking her back to Florida. John hoped that Chase's team could help them figure out what the FBI hadn't. Something was off. Colin wouldn't let things slide, but it sure as hell seemed like someone dropped the ball.

Elwood replied almost immediately. It was late, and he should have felt bad for disturbing him since they'd just gotten back from their deployment, but this was an emergency.

Pulling up his number, he dialed Elwood

and waited for him to pick up.

"Hey, Riot. What's up?"

"I need the team's help."

"Tell me what's going on."

"It's complicated."

"When isn't it?" Elwood chuckled. "It's the story of our lives, isn't it?"

"Ain't that the truth."

"Does it have anything to do with that woman you were tailing?" If John wondered about Elwood's powers of observation, he had his answer.

"Yes, it has everything to do with her. But I haven't been watching her since I was reactivated. She has an FBI team for protection but they're doing a piss poor job. Her apartment was broken into tonight and it looks like an IED went off in there."

"Was she hurt?"

"No, thank God. She was at dinner with me."

"So that's how it is? It's not just a good deed then?"

"No, I don't know how it happened but I can't get her out of my mind."

"Tell me something I didn't already know.

You were like a high school kid with a crush. We had a bet as to how long it would take you to realize it."

"Are you shitting me?"

"Nope. Looks like Disco will be cashing in."

"Fucking unbelievable. So much for brotherhood."

"Aww c'mon. If it was Chow or Gus, you'd have jumped all over that bet," Elwood said.

John laughed, Elwood was right. He wasn't as connected with this team yet, but they were still brothers and always had each other's six. Which is why he knew he could count on them to help keep Ari safe.

"Does she know how you feel?"

"She knows, she doesn't believe it yet, but she knows."

"Okay, so what can we do to help?"

"Ari is in trouble. Her ex was stealing information for the Chinese Ministry of State Security. He even tried to make it look like she was behind it all. The FBI has point, and my friend Colin is the SAC."

"Shouldn't they be handling this?"

"Yes, they should. The fucking trial is next week and they still don't have any leads. Her ex is keeping quiet, probably worried they'll come after him. But in the meantime, Ari's been getting threats and then tonight's break-in."

"What the hell have they been doing? Didn't I read in the paper about this over a year ago?"

"Yup. It doesn't make sense to me either. There's something else going on here. Earlier today she got an email with a picture of her and her friend on their balcony. It was taken maybe an hour before. The FBI couldn't trace the IP. Which seems fucked up. It's not the only time it happened either. No one is that good at covering their tracks. I sent Chase a text but it's the middle of the night in Florida."

"Your old team lead? Frost was his name, right?"

"Yeah. He has a couple of excellent computer guys working for him. I bet they can dig something up."

"Okay. Remember we can't operate on US soil. We'll have to turn it over to the FBI if we come up with anything."

"I know. I don't like it but I understand. Think you can all come over tomorrow around zero nine hundred and we'll put together a plan?"

"Sure, just make sure you keep Ariana in the loop. If you don't, it'll be the fastest relationship ever."

"I know, I'll talk to her."

"Night," Elwood said as he disconnected the call. John could have sworn he heard a female voice at Elwood's just before he hung up. Interesting.

"Talk to me about what?" Ari asked from behind him.

Shit. How much had she heard? Did she know he knew everything that had been going on with her? He had a feeling his ass about to be grass. Turning around, Ari stood in the doorway with her hands on her hips and Mr. Darcy parked at her feet. It didn't look like a happy pose. It looked like he was toast, but how burnt was the question.

"Just that I was calling in my team and my old boss. He's got a security firm in Florida with a couple of awesome computer geeks. I figured they might be able to help."

"Help what?"

"I'm hoping he'll have them take a look at your computer to track down the person sending the emails. Hopefully, it will lead to who's behind this."

"How do you know about the emails?"

Shit. He should have told her at dinner. It would have been better before all this other shit happened tonight. Now he had no choice but to tell her everything and hope she didn't walk out of his life. He'd promised to keep her safe and he would. Even if she never wanted to see him again. Maybe a partial truth would work?

"Colin told me about them while you were grabbing your stuff." He felt like a shit lying to her, but her safety was all that mattered.

"Why would he do that?"

"Because I told him I was going to protect you and I needed to know what was going on."

"I guess it helps that you've known him for years, right?"

"Not really. FBI agents don't like to share. I told him you were important to me, and in order to keep you safe, I had to know what could be a problem." Trying to prove that he was a better man than Chen and lying to her about knowing her truths was not the best way to do it.

"You told him that?"

"Yes, I did. I don't plan on hiding it anymore."

"I told you how I feel about relationships, and that I didn't want another one."

"Easy, Baby. You told me that after I'd already told him. So let's just take this one step at a time. I'm willing to take it slow, as slow as you need. Just don't shut me out."

She stared at him so intently he wondered if she could see into his soul. He struggled not to squirm. That's what lying did to him. He prayed it wouldn't bite him on the ass later. It was taking her too long to say something, but thankfully Mr. Darcy nudged her hand and whimpered. Damn, he loved that dog.

"You too? Is this a conspiracy?"

"Woof."

"No, it's not. But he knows I'm telling the truth." At least about that, his stomach churned, the acid roiling over the truths he hadn't shared.

"Neither of you make it easy. You realize that, right?"

"The last thing I want is to make things harder on you. But Colin hasn't been able to get to the bottom of this. I figured it wouldn't hurt if we took a shot."

"That's true. If you can find out who's behind all of this maybe I can have my life back."

"Exactly. See, it's all good."

"We'll see. Don't go getting cocky."

John laughed, and his hands itched to hold her. "Can I kiss you again?"

"Yes. No. Ugh, I don't know. Are you finished making your calls?"

"For tonight, yes. I have to wait to hear back from Chase. He's in Florida and he probably won't get back to me until tomorrow. So what about that kiss? I'm dying to taste you again."

Her cheeks turned bright pink as his words sank in. Seeing the color spread across her face was like seeing watercolor spread across paper, and it stirred his desire every time.

Still standing in the archway of the living room, Ari hadn't moved at all. Unable to resist his need for a kiss, he took a step toward her. When she didn't move or offer any objection, he crossed the rest of the room and stopped in front of her.

"If you don't want me to kiss you, you'd better tell me now." One heartbeat passed and then another. He tilted her face up to him with the tip of his finger and gasped at the glittering desire filling her eyes.

Drawing her to him, he slid his hands through her soft curls and then down her slender neck until his palms rested on her shoulders. Taut with tension, he kneaded them until it eased and she relaxed into his embrace.

"Ari, I promise I will keep you safe," he whispered as he lowered his lips to hers. His tongue coaxed them open allowing him inside to savor her sweetness. Drawn to her like a bee to honey, he couldn't imagine ever having enough of the luscious woman in his arms. Convincing her to give in to the feelings that were reflected in her eyes wouldn't be an easy task. But all of that could wait until she was safe.

When she slid her arms around his waist and her small hands clasped his back to hold him closer, a surge of satisfaction raced through him. Cradled against him, there was no way she didn't feel the erection pushing at his zipper. When she ground against him, he groaned into her mouth. As much as he wanted to pick her up and carry her into his bedroom it was much too soon. Making love to her right now would be wrong, and as much as his body

screamed to be inside her, his brain won out
—barely.

"What's wrong?"

"Absolutely nothing. Can't you feel how
much I want you?"

"Yes, that's why…"

"Shh," he said as he put his finger over her
soft lips. "I don't want you to have any regrets
when we make love. And I want our first time to
be as perfect as possible."

"I wouldn't…"

"Maybe not, but I'm not willing to take that
chance. I'm in this for the long run. You've told
me you don't want a relationship. Until that
changes, I'll wait."

"Are you serious?" her voice was filled
with doubt.

"I'm always serious, and it's killing me. I
want you more than I've wanted anyone in my
life, but I will wait until you're ready. You mean
too much to me to risk throwing it away."

"How is it even possible? You barely
know me."

"I know it feels that way, but it's been five
months, and I can't get you out of my mind.
No, we haven't really dated but I've seen you

every day when I'm not on a mission. I can't explain it, you're meant to be mine."

Her eyes widened at his explanation and he wanted to kick himself. The last thing he'd wanted to do was freak her out. He sucked at explaining emotions, and it was one of the reasons it had been easy to avoid relationships. But since his near-death experience, his outlook on life changed. And then he'd met her in the workout room. It was like being struck by lightning. In so many ways, he'd wished he'd met her under different circumstances, ones where he could have been honest with her.

"What if I want to have sex?"

"Do you?"

"I don't know." At least she was telling the truth, it was written all over her face.

"Exactly. Until you do know, no sex, but that doesn't mean we can't cuddle, kiss and enjoy each other's company."

"Okay."

She was lucky his phone rang, or she'd have seen just how much fun cuddling would be with him. Instead, he pulled the phone out of his pocket. It was Chase. He hadn't expected to hear from him until the morning.

"It's my old team leader."

"The one who lives in Florida?"

"Yeah."

"Do you want me to leave?"

John shook his head no as he answered the call. "Chase, thanks for getting back to me. But it's late there, tomorrow would have been fine."

"Your message sounded urgent."

"It still could have waited until morning."

"You've got me now, so tell me what's going on."

"I have Ari here with me, I'm going to put you on speaker. It's her story so she can fill in any blanks."

"Hi, Ari. I'm sorry you're going through all this," Chase's deep-voice echoed in the small kitchen.

"Hi Chase, John's told me a little about you. Thank you for helping me."

"It's what we do. So, what can I help with from three thousand miles away?"

"Actually, we'll probably need help from Alex and Rock. They're your computer dudes, right?" John said as he grinned at Ari, hoping to keep her calm.

"Yes, they're both top-notch."

"We're hoping they can figure out where some emails have come from."

"That's kid stuff. No problem. You mean the FBI couldn't do it?" Chase sounded as surprised as John was when Colin told him.

"That's what I've been told. It seems weird but they haven't been able to so far. Do you think they can remote into her computer and look around? We'll also forward the emails."

"No need to forward them, they'll take a look when they get in there."

"Great, I appreciate it. Is it going to be a problem to do it tomorrow since it's Saturday?"

"It shouldn't be. I'll text you in the morning and we'll set up a time. If Alex can't do it then Rock will. Either way, we'll figure it out."

"Thank you, Chase. I really appreciate it," Ari said, sounding like herself again.

"It's what we do for family and John is like family to me. Ariana, can you tell me what's going on?"

John grinned. "Thanks again, Chase. I hope Faith isn't ready to take my head off since I bothered you on a Friday night."

"No worries, she's used to this."

CHAPTER 8

"Call me Ari, most people do. Are you sure you want to help? You're probably going to be sorry when you hear about the mess I'm in."

"Riot filled me in on what he knows. Something to do with your ex-boyfriend? But I'd rather you tell me what you know."

"Yes, it was my ex. Apparently. I'm a pretty poor judge of character. He was stealing information for the MSS. I can't believe I was so stupid…" Just thinking about it made her want to curl up in a ball and hide.

"Hey, none of that. These people are trained to hide in plain sight. It would have been almost impossible to know what he was doing.

Don't beat yourself up, Baby," John said as he pulled her onto his lap.

It should have seemed weird, but it didn't. Then again, she'd been secretly mooning over him for months, so it was more like a dream come true. If only Paul hadn't ruined her life.

As she squirmed to get comfortable John moaned. A flush of satisfaction heated her cheeks. Knowing she'd turned him on made her feel a little better. After finding out Paul was only using her for access to her top-secret work, she wondered if she was attractive to men at all.

"He's right, Ari. You weren't the only person he deceived. Try and remember that," Chase said.

"Maybe not, but I was the person he tried to frame."

"Riot mentioned that but he didn't have any details. Can you fill us in?"

Ari turned her head to look at John. He nodded his encouragement. She wondered if he'd change his mind about her when he realized how stupid she'd been.

"He asked me out about three years ago. We both worked for the same contractor on base and we saw each other a lot at meetings and company functions. But we didn't work on any of the same projects, most of mine were and are classified."

"What happened after you started dating? Was there anything suspicious about his behavior at that time?"

"Nothing that I can remember. We didn't move in together until about a year after that. In the beginning, everything was great. He was great, everything a woman could want. That should have been the first indication something wasn't right."

John rubbed his hand up and down her back as she spoke. It was encouraging and comforting. It also made her sad. If she could only have met him before all this crap, they might have had a chance at something. But now she was probably a threat to his career as well as her own.

"When did it change?" Chase asked.

"Probably about six months later." Ari couldn't stay still any longer. She needed to move around, to wring her hands, to do anything but be surrounded by John's arms. Dredging up the past reminded her how naïve she'd been, which quickly changed to aggravation and then embarrassment.

The comforting words didn't matter. When it came down to it, she was just as much to blame as Paul. Ari had been through months of training and paperwork to get her top-secret clearance. It still amazed her that she'd only been on probation for six months before they cleared her. She should have lost her job or at least her clearance. Then she'd really have been screwed.

Mr. Darcy's head rubbed against her leg and surprised her. She hadn't realized he'd gotten up. It was amazing how in sync they were. He was the best thing that had happened since this mess started, well him and John. She didn't know what she'd done to deserve them but she couldn't have been more thankful they were there, for as long as it lasted.

"Ariana, baby?" John's voice startled her, she'd been lost in her own little world.

"What happened next, Ari?" Chase's voice was kind, like John's.

"Just little things that made me wonder about him. Going out alone to meet up with friends I didn't know. Lots of phone calls. If I was in earshot he'd hang up and go outside. It was just weird."

"Okay…" John prompted when she stopped talking. She hated rehashing the whole thing. It would have been easier to have Colin explain it all.

"I thought he was cheating on me. I asked him and he denied it. After that, the calls weren't as frequent and he stayed home in the evenings for a couple of weeks. Then it all started again."

"Did you ever find out who he was talking to?"

"Nope, never. It wasn't until the FBI questioned me that I realized it wasn't his regular phone that the calls were on. It was different, not a smartphone. I have no idea why I didn't realize it at the time."

"Do you know if the FBI got both of his phones?"

"I have no idea. They weren't very friendly at the beginning, they assumed I was the one stealing the information. They didn't even come for Paul. They scared the shit out of me when they burst into the apartment and cuffed me."

She'd been rubbing Mr. Darcy's fuzzy head

for comfort. When she stopped he licked her hand and she smiled. Thankfully, he hadn't let any rip since they'd been at John's. But she knew it was only a matter of time, and that made her smile. Maybe she did have an evil streak.

"Okay. Go on," Chase prodded.

"Around that time, I caught him at the computer in my office. He said he was just leaving me a note. I asked why he didn't just send a text or call, he said he'd hoped to see me too. But I didn't believe him. And after he left there wasn't a note anywhere. I didn't notice anything wrong with the computer and it had been locked down so I figured it was okay. The FBI said he'd attached a device that recorded my keystrokes. It was on the back of the computer console under the desk and I never saw it."

"When was that?" Chase asked, he sounded half distracted but from the clickety-clack of the computer keyboard he had to be taking notes.

"I think about six months before the FBI arrested me. I'd been thinking about breaking up with him. I'd even talked to my friend Shira about it. But before I had a chance it all blew up."

A low whistle came over the phone. "Holy shit, stole classified information for over six months?"

"Yes, that's what the FBI thinks. He almost got away with it. I was lucky he was an idiot or he'd have made it to China and I'd never been cleared."

"If the information came from you, how did they figure out it was him?" Chase asked.

"While I was in custody they searched our apartment. They found a false wall in the back of the closet with a couple of flash drives and a computer. Thank God his fingerprints were the only ones all over them."

"Eventually, they probably would have figured it out. Someone would have done a deep enough dive into his background and realized they'd made a mistake. But you'd have spent too much time locked up before they figured it out. Did he have the same access you did?" John said.

"No, not any top secret or even secret clearance. The FBI is convinced that's why he pursued me. So he could get access to my computer." Explaining the nightmare she'd lived for the last year made her sick to her stomach. How could she have been so naïve?

"Chase, Ari is exhausted and she looks about ready to fall over. You should have plenty to start with. We can pick this up tomorrow."

"Yes, I've got plenty. I'm sorry if I pushed you too hard. You've sure as hell been through hell and back. My team and I will get to the bottom of this with Riot's help. Just stay strong."

"Thank you. I really appreciate it."

"Night. Riot, I'll call you in the morning after Alex and Rock have had a chance to do some digging."

"Thanks, I appreciate it. Say hi to Faith for me."

"Will do."

John disconnected the call and wrapped his arms around Ari. She'd been pacing back and forth across the living room. With him behind her and Mr. Darcy in front, it was like being cocooned in happiness. She'd be lying if she didn't admit she liked it.

"Do you hate me now?"

"Why would I hate you?" John turned her in his arms and tipped her chin up to meet his eyes.

"Because you spend your life fighting to keep our country safe from people like me, people who expose our secrets to foreign countries."

"You didn't do any of that. The asshole Chen did. He picked you for a reason, your clearance. They should never have hired him in the first place. A solid background check should have set off all kinds of flags. You did nothing wrong."

"But…"

"Nope. Let me ask you this. Did you ever leave your computer unlocked?"

"No."

"Did you give him your password, or leave it where he could find it?"

"No."

"Did you ever bring classified information home on a non-government computer?"

"No."

"Then you did nothing wrong. He could have added that device on anyone's computer, but you had the information someone wanted. Now we have to find out who wanted it."

"Do you really think Chase's team can find out who is behind all of this?"

"If there is anyone in the world who can, it would be them, especially since the FBI's cyber team seems to be clueless for some reason."

"That makes me feel a teensy bit better."

"Good. Why don't you get changed and I'll pour us some wine? We can watch a movie and relax. How does that sound?"

"Great. But Mr. Darcy needs to go for a walk first."

"Okay, I'll take him. You're not leaving the apartment, remember? Unless we want your protection team breathing down our necks."

"Oh crap. I forgot. I'm sorry you're stuck with all of this. Do you mind taking him?"

"Of course not, we get along great, don't we, buddy?"

A low "woof" followed by the thumping of Mr. Darcy's tail against the wood floor made it clear John was right.

"Okay, but remember, Mr. Darcy, you better behave or we'll be tossed into a safe house with mean strangers."

As if he understood exactly what she'd said, he licked her hand and she'd swear he smiled at her. Dogs don't smile, do they?

John chuckled, kissed the side of her neck

and then went to find Mr. Darcy's leash. Did he really believe what he said? That she wasn't to blame. If she could convince herself she wasn't at fault, maybe she'd be able to get rid of the guilt she carried around. Who knew how many innocent lives were in danger because of the stolen information. Living with the knowledge that someone could have been hurt or worse had been eating her alive for the last eight months.

Mr. Darcy nudged her and licked her hand. "It's okay, I know you love me. And I love you more than anything." She bent to kiss him on the head as John returned.

"Hold on, you love the dog more than anything? Where does that leave me?"

"Sloppy seconds?"

"Eww, make that stinky seconds, maybe. No more buttered bread for you, Darcy. That's a horrific smell you let loose."

Ari couldn't stop laughing. The look on John's face as he wrinkled his nose was hysterical. He was right though, it was a ripe one. But in all fairness, it's not like he hadn't known Mr. Darcy was a fart cannon when he invited them to stay.

"I better get him outside before he lets something besides a toxic gas balloon loose in here."

She was still giggling as John dropped a soft kiss on her lips and took the dog for a walk.

Yellow crime scene tape crisscrossed the door to Ari's apartment and Mr. Darcy whimpered as they walked past. John understood, their girl was in danger and they needed to make sure she stayed safe.

"It's okay, boy. We'll make sure nothing happens to her."

He hadn't been worried about leaving her alone in the apartment. Colin had added an extra agent to her detail. Besides the agent outside, there was one in the lobby of the building monitoring all access on and off their floor. She might be his woman, but she was the witness on Colin's case and he had to follow orders too. He understood but it still irked him.

Something Ariana had said to Chase made him wonder if the second phone was what the conspirators were after. It was worth a call to

Colin to check, because if the FBI didn't have the phone, then it was out there somewhere, and they needed to find it.

"Rogers."

"Hey, Ariana mentioned that Chen had a second phone. Does the FBI have it?"

"The second phone? I haven't heard anything about it. I guess you and Ari have been chatting. I'll double-check the files but when we picked him up he only had one phone and it was clean. Maybe that's what they were searching for?"

"That's what I was thinking. I don't think she remembered it until tonight when Chase and I were asking her to tell us what happened."

"Dammit, that's why we told her to keep a journal. So it would trigger memories like that."

"It's not like she did it on purpose. I'm betting the shock today might have knocked the memory loose."

"Maybe. I'll get back to you when I have an answer. And remember, you are only supposed to help keep her safe. You're not cleared for this investigation."

"Yeah, yeah. I know. But if we turn something up, I'm not going to ignore it."

Colin's sigh was audible over the phone and John smiled. He wasn't making it easy for his friend.

"I'm going to end up losing my badge. I should never have brought you in on this. It seemed harmless and would keep you out of trouble. But it's turned into one horrendous clusterfuck."

"You said it. And you need to remember you read me in. But I'm sure you'll keep your badge when we figure out who's behind this and you help bring them in."

"If, not when."

"When did your positivity go out the window?"

"A long time ago. You know the routine. It's hell out there. How much shit have you seen? It makes it hard to believe that anyone is good anymore."

"You need to take some time off, you sound burned out."

"Maybe. We'll see after this case. For now, let me call Landau and see what, if anything, he knows about the second phone."

"Okay, let me know."

"Will do. Watch your six."

"Always." Disconnecting the call, he waved to the agent sitting in his car and headed back inside after picking up Mr. Darcy's poop. "I sure hope this helps your digestive issues. Any more stink bombs like that last one and you'll be staying on the balcony."

"Woof."

"Yeah, well get over it."

"Woooooof."

"You can whine all you want. I think you do it on purpose."

Mr. Darcy wagged his tail and kept his woofs to himself as they headed back into the apartment building.

While he was out, Ariana had gotten changed, found a bottle of wine and a couple of glasses and was waiting on the couch. Even though he knew she'd be safe, he still breathed a sigh of relief seeing her waiting for him. It gave him the warm fuzzies and finally felt like home.

CHAPTER 9

The brightness of the early morning sunshine streaming through the window woke Ari. After opening her eyes and gazing around the room it took her a few moments to remember what happened and why she wasn't in her own bed. Thank goodness for the warm fuzzy body lying next to her. Mr. Darcy might as well be her security blanket.

Rubbing her eyes, she tried to remember how she got into bed. The last thing she remembered was sipping wine with John while they watched Deadpool. He must have carried her to bed after she fell asleep. It was the only thing that made sense.

How embarrassing. Until yesterday afternoon they'd been workout buddies and she'd been his plant sitter. Then one dinner and a break-in later she was falling asleep on his couch. God, she hoped she didn't drool.

It looked like a beautiful day. A long walk in the dog park with Mr. Darcy would be a perfect idea. Or was until she remembered that she was basically on house arrest. Maybe she could convince the Shadows to let her go. It's not like they wouldn't be with her and John too. She had no doubt that unless he had a mission he wouldn't let her out of his sight. Thinking about trying to wrangle her way out of the apartment made her snort. She could already see the looks on their faces.

As she got out of bed, Mr. Darcy gave her a look and rolled over. Tough life he had. Grinning, she grabbed her suitcase and put it on the edge of the bed. She hadn't unpacked last night hoping that she'd be able to go back home sooner rather than later. But after talking to John and Chase last night, she had to accept that it wouldn't be happening anytime soon.

Grabbing a change of clothing, she headed to the bathroom for a shower. The only sound was Mr. Darcy's snoring. John was probably sleeping. She'd forgotten that he'd just returned from his deployment yesterday and had to be exhausted.

Steam filled the small bathroom as she stood under the pulsing water. The heat and pounding of the water on her shoulders helped to ease some of the tension that had been her constant companion for the last year. For a few minutes, everything was right in the world. No problems to think about, just blissful quiet and the water beating on her body. A perfect way to start the day. The only thing better would be a cup of coffee on the counter waiting for her when she stepped out of the shower. But she hadn't even thought about making it.

Too bad that for the foreseeable future she'd be stuck in the apartment. The trial was still over a week away since it kept getting postponed. If she had to stay inside she'd go stir crazy. And just like that, the tension was back, and all the peaceful thoughts were gone, replaced by a dark cloud.

Dwelling on what she couldn't do wouldn't help her at all. She needed to think positive about this. She had Mr. Darcy with her and there was John. But thinking about him brought on an entirely different kind of tension. Spending so much time with him in his apartment. Oh. My. God. How was she going to keep her hands off of him? Just the few kisses they'd shared curled her toes.

Or maybe, that was the solution. He said he was interested. Her body was too. Could they have a fling to kill the time and then go their separate ways after the trial and she had her life back? She was sure when he told her he wanted to see where things would go he hadn't meant permanently. Why would he? If anything she'd be a liability to him.

Okay, maybe having sex with John was a bad idea. All of this stress was messing with her. Focus, Ari. Maybe Chase and his team would be able to figure out who Paul had been working with and this could all go away. If not, maybe WITSEC was the best option. It would be the only way she could truly protect the people she loved.

The shower renewed her energy even if the stress was already eating away at it. Coffee was calling her name. By the time she got to the kitchen, Mr. Darcy was right at her heels. And he almost knocked her over when she stopped short seeing John at the table drinking coffee and reading the paper.

"Morning, Baby. Did you and Mr. Darcy sleep well?"

"I did, I don't think I moved at all. I guess you had to put me to bed?"

"I think Mr. Darcy would have given it a gallant try but it would have been hard to lift you without hands."

"I'm sorry I fell asleep on you." Ari's embarrassment grew just thinking about him having to carry her into the bedroom and put her to bed. Thankfully she'd already been in her PJs.

"Don't worry about it. Yesterday was traumatic. I was surprised you lasted as long as you did. Neither one of us made it through the movie. We're a couple of party animals aren't we?"

"No kidding. You'd think we're an old married couple." As soon as the words left her lips she wished the floor would open up and suck her in. Where the hell had that thought even come from?

John got up from the table and smiled before leaning down to give her a kiss. It started out soft, gentle, but as soon as his tongue slid over her lips, she sucked him in, craving him like a starving person craved food. Sliding her arms around his waist, she pressed her body against him pressing his erection against her stomach. As she wriggled against him, he groaned into her mouth and pulled away. Again. Damn him and his rules. Why did he need commitment? Wasn't that supposed to be the woman's thing?

Vibrating with need, her desire made her hot and twitchy. Ari could count on one hand how many men she'd had sex with, but lack of experience or not, she'd never reacted to any man like she did to John. It was amazing, and when they finally made love she'd probably spontaneously combust.

"I could get used to waking up like this."

That's what scared her. She wanted him in every way imaginable, but it wasn't as simple as saying yes to him. Turmoil roiled in her stomach, were her feelings for *him*, or for the knight in shining armor riding to her rescue? Was she falling in love with him? As long as she was soul-searching, she had to admit that it sure felt like love. Until she knew for sure, it was a lot safer not to give in to her desire. The little devil on her shoulder laughed and wished her luck.

"How do you take your coffee?"

"I'll get it. It's enough you're letting me stay here, you don't have to wait on me."

"I want to. I didn't know if you ate breakfast. So after my run, I stopped and bought some bagels."

"Most of the time I just have coffee, but I won't turn down a bagel. Thank you," Ari said with a smile.

"How do you take it? Toasted? Butter or cream cheese?"

"Since they're fresh, just cream cheese. You're going to spoil me if you keep this up."

"Exactly. Is it working?" he asked with a huge smile. Grabbing a mug out of the cabinet, he filled it with coffee. "How do you take it?"

"Half and half if you have it or just milk and two sugars."

"Was that so hard?"

"Maybe," she said and stuck out her tongue.

"If you do that again I'll take it prisoner."

"How would you do that?" Flirting with him was too much fun and would get her into trouble if she wasn't careful.

"Stick it out again and you'll find out," he said and waggled his eyebrows. She liked this playful side of him and so did Mr. Darcy. The fuzzy pup was sitting at his side, with one paw on his knee begging for food.

"Mr. Darcy, get down. You know better."

"It's okay. It doesn't bother me. I grew up with a big dog who acted a lot like he does."

"Farts and all?"

"Okay, maybe not exactly like him." John laughed and patted the dog on the head. "Mr. Darcy is definitely the gassiest canine I've ever met." As if to make sure they didn't forget it, he let one rip. It wasn't silent and it was deadly, causing Ari's eyes to fill with tears from the stench.

"Mr. Darcy, you should be ashamed of yourself. I thought you did it because you didn't like Shira. Looks like there's a trip to the vet in your future. This can't be normal."

At the word vet, he laid down on the floor at John's feet and put his paws over his face. You couldn't tell her that he didn't understand what she said. Too bad she didn't have her phone. It would have been a perfect picture to add to her collection.

Where was her phone? Now that she

thought about it, she couldn't remember the last time she'd had it.

"Have you seen my phone?"

John opened the window to let out the stink and finished making her coffee. "No, I don't think so. When did you have it last?"

"That's just it, I don't remember. I'll be right back. I'm going to check my purse."

"Okay. We'll be here, me and Farty McFartface."

That was a worthy *Shira-ism* and she'd have to remember to tell her about John's new nickname for Mr. Darcy. So much happened since yesterday that she didn't know about, and she'd be hurt if Ari didn't tell her soon.

It was hard to believe that it *was* just yesterday. Damn. Finding out that Ari was staying with John would be a hell of a surprise. Knowing how Shira's mind worked meant she'd be giving Ari a ton of grief about not jumping his bones. Sex was definitely high on Shira's "you're missing out" list for Ari.

In the spare room, she grabbed her purse from the top of the dresser and dumped the contents onto the bed. The last thing to hit the bed was the missing phone. With a sigh of relief, she pushed the button to check for messages. Dead. And of course, she'd forgotten to grab her charger.

John was on his phone when she walked back into the kitchen. He'd been busy while she'd been searching for her phone. A mug of coffee, a sliced bagel, and a tub of cream cheese was on the table waiting for her. If he kept this up, she'd be spoiled rotten.

From what she could hear of his side of the conversation, he was talking to Chase or one of his guys. Not trying to eavesdrop, she took a bite of her bagel. Watching as John refilled his coffee, she smiled as he stepped back over the dog. It was crazy how fast he had adapted to her staying there. He'd even remember to check for Mr. Darcy sprawled on the floor.

"I haven't heard from Colin yet."

"What's taking so long?" Chase asked.

"No clue. There has to be something else going on. Unless he's leaving me out of the loop."

"If we ran our missions like this, we'd be in deep shit."

"Exactly. But we're not really supposed to be involved either. It's only because Ari is here he's sharing anything."

"Okay, well I think we should assume they didn't know about the other phone until you told them last night," Chase said.

"I think so too. Hold on, Ari is here now. I'll put you on speaker."

"Good morning, Ari," Chase asked.

"You guys start early, huh?"

"Mission or not I'm up at the crack of dawn and out running or in the gym. But it's also three hours later here."

"Oh right. I forgot about that."

"Most days I get up before dawn to do PT. After so many years of operating, it's a hard habit to break."

"My father did until the end," John added.

"I guess when you do it for so long it would be."

"Exactly. Anyway, the reason I called is that Alex found out a few things about Chen. He should never have been hired to work on any kind of government contracts. Paul Chen is an assumed name he began using about four years ago. He's done a good job covering his tracks, but it didn't take us too much to find out the truth. What I don't get is why your company and the FBI didn't discover any of this. His real name is Huang Chiu. He was born on mainland China and came to the U.S. fifteen years ago on a student visa. After he graduated he just disappeared, and there was no sign of him until he started using the Paul Chen alias. That's when he started interviewing with a number of government contractors."

"I told you Chase's team was good," John said as he refilled her coffee mug.

"Yes, you did. I can't believe you found all of this in a few hours. I'm like you, how did the FBI miss this? Paul didn't have any kind of a security clearance at work, so maybe they didn't bother to do a background check."

"I'm not sure, but when Colin calls Riot he can fill him in. Hopefully, they already knew but just didn't tell you. I can't imagine it wouldn't be part of their case against him," Chase said.

"I hope so. It still seems weird to me," Ari replied before taking another bite of her bagel.

"The FBI could have brought in Homeland

or the CIA. Especially if they found out Chen was using an alias. With all the different alphabet agencies things can get dicey."

"I guess so. But where does that leave me? Are we any closer to figuring out who he's working with?"

"Not yet, but Alex and Rock are hopeful they'll have more information by this afternoon."

"That would be great. I want all of this to be over already."

"Sit tight for a bit longer and we'll get to the bottom of this. Just stay close to Riot and he'll make sure you're safe."

"I will. I don't think he'd give me a choice," she said and stuck her tongue out at John. "Please thank your team for me. It almost feels like there is light at the end of the tunnel."

"It is, Baby, it's only a matter of time," John said as he reached for her hand across the table. "It will be okay, you'll see."

"Okay, gotta run. Talk to you later. Riot make sure you watch your six," Chase said as he disconnected the call.

"Do you really think Chase's team will

uncover information that the FBI didn't?" Ari asked as she refilled her coffee.

"Yes, I do. I'm not sure what's going on with the FBI. It could be that they do know all about Chen and kept it to themselves. It wouldn't surprise me either."

"That's true. Colin told me that they aren't obligated to share any information with me."

"Right, besides with the trial coming up, they probably don't want to risk showing their hand. But I know we'll get to the bottom of it. Chase was a SEAL too and we don't give up."

"Pretty sure of yourself, aren't you?"

"Hell yeah I am, I'm a SEAL."

"Is that your standard answer?"

"Pretty much. There usually isn't a better one." John laughed as she rolled her eyes. He loved teasing her, it was almost as fun as kissing her. Just the memory of the softness of her lips made him wonder what it would be like to slide his fingers over her skin. And instant hard-on. Dammit. If she stayed with him much longer, he was going to need to buy some looser jeans.

"I still can't believe they discovered all of that about Paul since last night."

"With any luck, they'll figure out the rest of

the puzzle before the weekend is over." He was able to read Ari well enough to know that she was afraid to hope that this would all end soon. Not that he could blame her since it had been going on for over a year. No wonder she was afraid to get close to anyone.

"Do you think we can take Mr. Darcy to the dog park. It's such a beautiful day and he'd love it."

Hearing his name, the fluffy stinkball's tail thumped against the floor. He did his growly speak that sounded more like a combination of a low moan and a series of woofs. He was quite the talker—from both ends. It was like karma had given Ariana a gift for all the shit it put her through. The dog was so well-behaved he had to belong to someone who'd loved him before he ended up at the shelter.

"I'm not sure your jailors will agree, but we can try. I took him out while you were sleeping, but I'm sure he needs to go again. I'll take him while you finish your breakfast."

"You don't mind? It's sure easier than dealing with the Shadows. Oh, before you go, do you have a charger I can borrow? My phone is dead, and I didn't pack mine. With the mess in my apartment, I probably wouldn't have found it anyway."

"Let me get mine and we'll see if it will work." Grabbing his charger from his bedroom, he brought it into the kitchen. "Here you go," he said and handed her his charger. "If it doesn't fit, Mr. Darcy and I can pick up a new one on our walk."

"Thank you," Ari said as she took the cord.

Without thinking, he dropped a kiss on her forehead as she slid by him to plug her phone into the charger.

"Yay. It works."

"Excellent. One less thing to worry about."

"In case I didn't tell you last night, thank you for letting us stay with you. I don't even want to think about having to be in some strange place with the Shadows watching every move I make."

"You're welcome. I'm glad you're here, although the safe house might have been a better idea. There is still the chance you'll need to go into Witness Protection, okay? I'll do my best to make sure that doesn't happen, but we don't even know who we're dealing with right now." Just saying the words made John's insides twist into knots. He couldn't lose her now, not to whoever Chen was working with, or to WITSEC.

"With you and Chase's team working on it, I'm going to take some of your confidence and believe it will all work out."

"Baby, I love that you're putting your trust in us, but there always need to be backup plans. As a SEAL, I learned that you need a Plan B, C, D, and maybe E too."

"Really? Your missions are that disorganized?"

"We're not talking about me. I'm trying to make sure you stay safe." John shook his head. Her stubborn streak was almost as bad as his. Trying to reason with her was like talking to a brick wall. It would make for some interesting arguments. But afterward, they'd make up, and he'd enjoy every minute of it.

CHAPTER 10

After John left to take Mr. Darcy for a walk, Ari cleared the breakfast dishes. While waiting for them to get back, she got her journal and sat at the kitchen table to write about the day before. Journaling had really helped her over the last year, not just to remember details she would need when she testified, but to remind her that she had something to be grateful for every day. There had been so many, especially after she'd been arrested when she needed that reminder. If Colin hadn't suggested it for writing down everything she could remember about Paul, she'd never had found this release.

There were times when the blank white

page taunted her, like today. When there were so many emotions and thoughts that she had trouble getting them out of her head and onto the paper. As she tapped her pen on the notebook, she contemplated where to begin. Yesterday had been amazing and horrible. Shira's visit had been fun even with all her pushing. Then the dinner with John. Talk about knocking her off her feet. It made her feel normal for the first time in ages. But the threatening email and complete destruction of her apartment turned it into a nightmare.

Ari poured another cup of coffee and decided she should focus on the good things first. Beginning with Shira's visit, she'd written a couple of words when her cell phone rang. It was her bestie's ringtone. Talk about timing.

"Hey, girl. I was going to call you as soon as my phone finished charging."

"Ms. Nelson, you're not an easy person to reach."

"Who is this? Why do you have my friend's phone?" Panic made her shake. Why did they have Shira's phone? Was she hurt or worse? Bile rose in her throat. It took every bit of willpower she had to swallow it down and listen over the pounding in her ears.

"You're wasting time. Stop talking. She is fine for now. As long as you do as I ask nothing will happen to her. But if you don't follow my instructions that will change."

Ari's mind raced as she tried to figure out if she recognized the voice. It was definitely male, and he had a heavy accent that was really similar to Paul's.

"Before I agree to anything, I need to know Shira's alive. Let me talk to her and I'll do whatever you want." The silence on the other end made her grip the phone tighter and a chill slide down her spine. It was taking him too long to answer. Praying she hadn't pushed him too hard; she breathed a sigh of relief when she heard Shira's voice.

"Ari?

"Oh my God, are you okay?"

"Yes, but what the hell is…"

It wasn't much but she'd heard her voice. Assholes.

"As I said, your friend is alive. If you want her to stay that way, you need to bring me the micro SD card Chen gave you."

"I don't know what you're talking about. He never gave me a memory card."

"Wrong answer. We know he gave it to you. I will call tomorrow and tell you where to bring it. If you want to see your friend alive you'd better find it. Don't tell the FBI anything, or your SEAL boyfriend either."

"But I..." The line went dead before she could say anything else. The FBI had her phone under surveillance. Whoever the guy was he probably knew and kept the call short to keep it from being traced. It seemed like they had inside information all the time. They knew way too much.

The FBI swept her apartment weekly for listening devices. So far they hadn't found any. Now that Mr. Darcy was there all day, she couldn't imagine anyone getting in without someone finding out. She'd drawn the line at cameras in her apartment, she had to have some privacy.

Something was definitely off, but right now her focus needed to be on rescuing Shira. Even if she could find the SD card, she'd be damned if she'd give it to them. They had enough top secret information from Paul. There had to be some way to do this where they thought they were getting the information and she and Shira could get away. But how?

It was a risk since they'd told her not to, but she had to tell John. But she'd make him swear not to tell Colin. If the FBI got involved she'd never see Shira alive again, she knew it without a doubt. Maybe his friend Chase could help. The next problem was the card. Even if Paul had put it somewhere, had she brought it from their old apartment when she moved to this building? Trying to find it in the mess they'd left her would be almost impossible and she had her doubts that it was there. She didn't remember seeing Paul with any memory cards.

When John and Mr. Darcy got back from their walk, she was pacing back and forth in the kitchen. She must have looked terrible because as soon as she met his eyes, he wrapped her in a huge bear hug.

"Are you okay? What happened?"

"If I tell you, you have to promise not to tell Colin."

"What? Why?" His body stiffened against hers. Was he mad at her?

"Promise me and I'll tell you." Ari prayed

he'd agree. If he didn't she wasn't sure what she'd do.

"Okay, but I'm not happy about it."

"You're going to be less happy when I tell you."

"That's what I'm afraid of. C'mon, let's go sit on the couch."

Following him into the living room with Mr. Darcy at her side she felt a little better. Less shaky, knowing that she wouldn't have to do this alone. Or at least she hoped she wouldn't.

Pulling her onto his lap, he wrapped his arms around her. She should have objected but it helped her feel safe. Mr. Darcy jumped onto the couch and laid against her legs.

"Tell me what happened after I left with Mr. Darcy."

"Nothing at first, but my phone rang. I thought it was Shira, but it wasn't."

"What do you mean?"

Tears gathered in her eyes and throat, and she was having trouble getting the words out. She hated crying. Clearing her throat, she wished she had a glass of water. "It was someone else, but he had Shira's phone."

"What did he say?"

"That he had Shira and would hurt her unless I did what he asked. He wants me to bring him a micro SD card Paul supposedly gave to me. But I can't remember him doing that. Nothing even remotely like a memory card."

"Are you sure? Maybe it was something he asked you to hold on to for him."

"No, nothing like that. After we got the apartment and moved in together, he didn't give me anything except flowers once in a while. I don't want Shira to die. Oh my God, what are we going to do? I can't let anything happen to her…"

"Breathe. Slowly. In and out. It's going to be fine. We'll get Shira back."

"Promise?"

He winced. It was a promise he couldn't make. No one could.

"I know you can't. I'm sorry, I shouldn't have asked."

"I promise I'll do my best, Baby," John said and kissed the top of her head as he squeezed her.

Even Mr. Darcy tried to comfort her. Moving closer, he put his fluffy head on her leg and looked up at her with his big brown eyes. It melted her heart and she ruffled his ears.

"I'm okay. It was just a shock getting the call. I'm sorry I fell apart."

"You have nothing to be sorry for. You've been going through hell for what, a year? Now, this? I'd worry about you if you weren't upset."

Leaning into his chest, Ari took a deep breath and inhaled the scent that was pure John, clean and fresh like the outdoors. Being close to him did make her feel better but relying on him would take more trust than she was able to give him yet.

"I need to get into my apartment and search for it."

"How about we call Chase first and see if he's uncovered anything?"

"That won't help. And it hasn't been that long since he called." It was clear he didn't want her to go to her apartment and he was looking for reasons to stall. It didn't make sense to her. There wasn't any danger there now. They wanted her to find the card.

"Humor me, okay? We'll tell him about the phone call and see if he has anything else. If he doesn't, we'll search your apartment."

After the full plate of emotions she'd been through for the last hour, she gave in easier than she should have. But waiting another five or ten minutes probably wouldn't make a difference. Trying to find that little memory card would be like looking for a needle in a haystack.

"Fine, but after the call, I'm going to check the apartment with or without you. I'm not leaving the building so the Shadows won't need to know."

"Maybe, we'll see how close they're monitoring you. But you're right, it shouldn't trigger any phone calls to Colin."

The last thing John expected when he returned with Mr. Darcy was Ari pacing back and forth in the kitchen, her face pale and her cell phone clenched in her hand. Without thinking, he took her in his arms. As soon as he touched her, his protective instincts kicked into full blast. The need to keep her safe was overwhelming.

After she explained the phone call, he had to restrain his anger. Whoever was behind this was starting to panic with the trial date approaching.

Why else would everything have escalated? Taking Shira was a bold move, but after they couldn't find the memory card in Ari's apartment they had limited options.

No way was he allowing her to bring anything to those guys, alone or otherwise. But he needed time to come up with a plan, which is why he suggested calling Chase first. Maybe he'd be able to help.

"Can I get you anything?"

"I'm okay."

"Bullshit. You're still pale as a ghost and shaking. Let me get you some water. Although whiskey would probably be better."

"Water would be good."

After sliding her off of his lap, he got up. "Mr. Darcy, stay with Ari. I'll be right back."

The dog wagged his tail and rearranged himself closer to her after she got settled. Dialing Chase's number as he got a glass of water for her, he tried to tamp down his anger. After he got done with Chase, his next call would be to Elwood. They were supposed to come over later, but he wanted to make sure she had plenty of protection now.

"Hey, Riot."

"Chase, we have a situation."

"What happened? Is Ari safe?"

"For now. Whoever is behind all of this kidnapped her friend, Shira. They want Ari to bring them a micro SD card they said Chen gave to her."

"Fuck me running. Does the FBI know?"

"Not so far, but it's only a matter of time since they have surveillance on her phone."

"How long ago did she get the phone call?"

"About an hour or so. I was walking Mr. Darcy. They called her on Shira's phone. Not sure how closely the FBI is paying attention."

"Pretty shitty if you ask me. They should have been in her apartment as soon as she hung up the phone."

"Agreed. Something weird is going on there. We've worked with the FBI before and I've never seen anything like this. Colin has mentioned a few times that he's getting all kinds of pushback from higher up the food chain."

"Okay. So what's the plan?"

"I was hoping you'd help me come up with one. There is no way I'm letting Ari walk in there…"

"It's not up to you," Ari said from behind him.

Turning, he met her eyes. Her color was back in her cheeks.

"It's too dangerous," John replied and clicked the speaker button on his phone and then handed her the glass of water.

"Hi, Ari. I'm really sorry to hear about your friend."

"Thanks, Chase. I just need to get her back no matter what John says. They said not to involve him or the FBI and that I needed to bring it by myself. If that's how I get Shira back, then that's what I'll do."

"You know it's a trap, right? Hell, they might just kill you on sight."

"Yes, it's a trap. That's why I told you, so we can come up with a plan to get Shira back without getting either of us killed."

"You've got a smart woman there," Chase said. "It won't be easy. About the only thing I can think of is to put a bug on you so we can track you."

"That's what I was thinking too," John said. "What if they have jammers?"

"We'd be dead in the water."

"I don't like the sound of that," Ari said.

John wrapped his arm around her and pulled her against his side. Mr. Darcy followed her and took his usual position at her feet.

"Are there any other options, Chase?"

"I don't think so. You said the FBI is monitoring her phone?"

"Yes, they are. At least that's what Colin told me," Ari said.

"And he still hasn't shown up at the apartment?" Chase asked.

"Nope. Weird right?"

"Very. Okay, let me talk to Rock and Alex. See if they have any more information on our friends. Hopefully, they're so desperate that they aren't planning properly and won't think about jammers. Especially if they told her not to bring anyone else in."

"Yeah. That's a possibility. I think they're freaking out now that the trial is next week. The last thing they want is confirmed evidence that can lead back to the upper levels of the Chinese MSS."

"It that what we think is going on?" Chase asked.

"When Colin first brought me in he let that little piece slip. So yeah."

Chase whistled. "That is big. Which makes it even weirder that the FBI isn't banging down your door to get to her right now."

"I'm right here. Please stop talking about me like I'm not," Ari said.

"Sorry, Baby." John had slipped into mission mode without even thinking. Troubleshooting was one of his strengths. "Too many missions, it just happens when I have a problem to work out."

"I understand but I don't have to like it."

"We'll try to be more cognizant of that, Ari. I'm sorry too. My wife, Faith, complains about the same thing," Chase added.

"I can't stand here doing nothing, I'm going to go and search my apartment for the memory card."

"Please wait for me," John said gently.

"Okay, you two go do what you need to. I'll call back after I talk to the rest of the team and see if they have any other ideas." Chase disconnected before either of them could say goodbye.

John turned so he was face-to-face with Ari and tilted her chin up so he could look into her eyes. "You know even if we find that card you can't give it to Shira's kidnappers, right?"

Expecting her to argue with him, he was surprised when she nodded in agreement.

"I know. But I'm hoping if I can find it, I can create a duplicate with fake information. They'll check the card so it can't be empty."

If possible his admiration jumped up a few thousand feet. She was beautiful and smart and had him wrapped around her little finger. It wouldn't be easy to try to keep her safe, that was obvious. She would fight him on not going to the drop off point, but he couldn't let her go. They'd find another way to get Shira back. What that was, he hadn't figured out yet.

"Finding it isn't going to be easy, especially in the huge mess they left after their search."

"I know. But we have to try. Now we know it exists, the FBI will definitely want it for their case."

"And what are you going to tell Colin when he shows up? It's only a matter of time until one of the idiots monitoring your calls realizes something is wrong." John still couldn't believe no one had shown up.

Laughing, Ari shook her head. "I'm glad he

hasn't come over. I don't want to lie to him, but I will if it's the only way to save Shira."

Again that iron wall of stubbornness reared its head. When she dug her feet in, the only way to move her was to pick her up. He was worried she'd try to outmaneuver him to save her friend.

"Let me just text my team and then we'll head over."

"Okay."

Her frustration was becoming more visible by the moment but racing over there wasn't going to help them find a little memory card any easier, the damn thing was about the size of a dime. Quickly sending a text off to Elwood with the latest intel and the location of her apartment, he tucked his phone back into his pocket.

"I think Mr. Darcy should stay here." He'd swear the dog gave him a dirty look and then laid down on the floor and put his paws over his face.

"You hurt his feelings," Ari said with a grin.

"Seriously?" And then he was hit with an invisible cloud of stink that almost knocked him over. "Does he do that on purpose?"

"Some think so."

"Well too bad, Darcy. It could be dangerous

for you over there. You'll stay here and guard the place," John said from behind his hand. He had to do something to block the stench.

Ari was in a full-blown giggle fit by this time and he just rolled his eyes at her. It made her focus on something other than her friend, and any distraction was a good one.

CHAPTER 11

U sing a hammer to remove the nails from the plywood that had been put up as a temporary door, they were able to get into her apartment. But a half-hour later, they hadn't found any sign of the memory card. Not that Ari expected they would. It was possible she had left it in their old apartment when she moved. Since he'd used a false wall in the closet to hide other items, the card could be just about anywhere, if it existed at all.

"Any luck," John asked as he came into the bedroom where she'd been searching.

"No, nothing. I guess you haven't found it either?"

"The mess they left isn't helping. I'm trying to put things back together as I search."

"Me too, but it's not helping. I wonder if it's even here. I could have left it behind without knowing, or maybe the slimy asshole was a double agent and he gave it to someone else."

John had been going through the mess of items near her vanity when he stopped and turned to look at her. "That would explain a lot."

"What do you mean?"

"Hold on," John said as he pulled out his phone and sent a text to someone. "Sorry, I wanted to let Chase know what you said. It would explain why the FBI has been so weird. Maybe he was working for them too."

"I don't think so. Then why did they arrest me?"

"To make all of this look good. Or if they wanted the MSS to think they were successful, but more likely the CIA was using him."

"And the FBI and CIA don't talk to each other?"

"Not usually. Two separate agencies and jurisdictions. But it still doesn't explain everything."

"What doesn't?" Colin asked as he appeared in her bedroom door. "And you shouldn't be in here. I know you saw the crime scene tape across the door before you pulled it down."

Ari and John exchanged glances. She hoped he'd know what to say because she didn't.

"Yeah we saw it. But Ali was getting antsy cooped up in my apartment. We figured it couldn't hurt to come over and pick up a few more of her things. Then we started cleaning up."

"Did you forget this is a crime scene? You need to get out of here."

Ari wasn't ready to leave yet. They still had so much to go through. But it didn't look like Colin would back down, so she'd have to sneak back over later.

"Can I just grab some more clothing?"

"Okay but touch as little as possible. Until you get word we've released the crime scene you need to stay out of here," Colin said in the authoritative FBI voice he used when he tried to make sure she'd listen to him. It didn't work on her, but he wasn't ready to give up on it yet. The last time was when she snuck out of the apartment to visit Mr. Darcy before the adoption was final. There had been hell to pay when she got home, but it had been worth every minute.

"John, can you get me a bag from the kitchen?" She hoped he realized what she was trying to do, which was to get him and Colin out of the room for a bit. She wanted to check one more place before she grabbed some of her underwear and a few more shirts.

"No problem. C'mon Colin, I have a few things I want to run by you."

After a short hesitation and giving her the stink eye, he followed John. Knowing she didn't have much time before they got back, she grabbed her jewelry box from where she'd just noticed it on the floor by her dresser. It didn't look like much, just an old shoebox she'd covered with scrapbook paper. It was her grandmother's idea. They'd decorated it when she was ten and spent the summer with her. Over the years, it had worn out in places and Ari covered it in clear packing tape to help hold it together. The box was one of the possessions she treasured, and Paul knew it too. If he'd hidden the memory card anywhere, there was a good chance it was in the box.

It had been a while since she'd opened the

box and gone through her treasures. Most of the jewelry was cheap costume stuff she'd picked up over the years. Every piece had meaning though and she had to remind herself she didn't have time for a walk through the memories.

Quickly sifting through the contents, she was both relieved and disappointed that the card wasn't there. If he'd put it in there it would have tainted her memories, but it also meant she had no idea where he could have hidden the damn thing.

"Is one bag enough?" John asked as he made his way through the apartment to the bedroom.

Grateful for the warning, she closed the box and shoved it under the dresser. Then grabbed a few shirts and underwear and bras. "Yes, that should work. More clothing means I won't have to do laundry as often."

A few seconds later they appeared in the doorway. "Do you have what you need now?" Colin asked.

"Yeah, this should hold me for a few more days."

"Great. Let's get back to John's apartment, we have a few things to discuss."

It sounded kind of ominous, and Ari's stomach turned over. Did he know about Shira and the missing memory card?

Filling the bag with her clothing, she followed them out of the apartment and Colin waited for John to nail the plywood back into place.

"Stay out of the apartment," Colin said as he dropped the keys into her palm.

Ari didn't say a word and she was grateful that he hadn't asked her to promise. She'd have been screwed then.

John looked like he was about to say something but stopped when he saw his team coming down the hallway to meet us. Ari breathed a sigh of relief. The SEALs would hopefully distract Colin from giving her more grief.

"You must be Ari, I'm Elwood, and this is Shaggy, Gus, and Disco."

"Hi. It's great to meet you, although I kind of feel like I know you already from John's stories."

"Don't worry, I didn't tell her all of your

deep dark secrets," John said when Elwood raised his eyebrows and glanced at him.

"Good thing or we have quite a few stories we could share with Ari about you."

"It's great you're having a meet and greet, but can we move this into John's apartment?"

The grouchier Colin got the more Ari decided it had nothing to do with Shira or the memory card. It made her think about her bestie and what she must be going through. They'd better keep their word and not hurt her. Thinking about it made her want to throw up.

Leading the way to his apartment, John and his teammates chatted, leaving her and Colin to walk together.

"I'm surprised you left the fartbag behind."

"Huh?" Ari had been thinking about Shira and not paying attention to whatever Colin had been saying. "I'm sorry, what?"

"Your dog? I'm surprised you don't have him with you."

"I figured it was safer to leave him behind. There's broken glass on the floor."

"So it wasn't to keep the crime scene from getting messed with?"

"No, I'm sorry. But seriously, it's my apartment. The investigators were there half the night. What's going on? You're not usually this cranky." As soon as the words were out of her mouth, she wished she could take them back. But it was too late.

"You think I'm cranky? I'm trying to do my job, to keep you safe, and you do everything you can to make it harder. I should just take you and put you in the safe house and leave you there until the trial."

She'd poked a raw nerve. He was right, she hadn't made it easy. But for the last year, she'd had to put up with constant surveillance, being called in for depositions, meetings, and interviews with different agents. In the beginning, she'd had to deal with reporters too. That had been the worst part. They'd reported she was stealing secret documents. Of course, when she was cleared they were nowhere around to report that story.

"I'm sorry. I don't know what else to say."

"No, I'm sorry. It can't be easy on you either. We'll talk about it inside. Okay?" Colin said in a much less irritated tone.

∽

If the jumping up and down tail wagging was any indication, Mr. Darcy was thrilled to see Ari and a bunch of new people to sniff and lick. John grinned at the thought of the inevitable stink bomb he'd let loose. With any luck, it would be in Colin's direction. He'd been an ass since he showed up at Ari's apartment. When he took him into the kitchen to give Ari time to look for the card, he'd ripped him a new one for letting her go into the apartment. Something was definitely eating at him. In all the time they'd been friends, he'd never seen him act like this.

"I need to speak to Ari alone," Colin announced after they were inside the apartment.

John glanced in her direction to try to see what she was thinking, but he couldn't. She looked upset, which was expected considering how Colin treated her, but that was as much as he could determine. "Do you want me to come to? We can go into the kitchen. The guys will stay here."

The SEALs nodded in agreement.

"I don't think that's necessary," Colin answered.

"I'd like him to. You might as well let him. If you don't I'll just tell him later," Ari said.

"Alright. C'mon then."

Following behind Ari and Colin, John turned to the guys. "We'll be back in a couple of minutes."

They nodded their understanding. No one wanted Colin to know how much his teammates had been read about what was going on, or that Chase's guys were involved. From the way he'd been acting, it would turn into a huge clusterfuck.

"We're alone now, so do you want to tell us what the fuck has your panties in a twist? I've never seen you be this much of an asshole," John asked.

"You're asking me that after where I found you? You're supposed to keep her protected…"

"Enough of this pissing contest. You're friends, right? So cut it out. It's obvious something happened, like John said, because you're not usually this wound up," Ari interrupted.

Colin sighed. "There's been a new development."

It couldn't be about the memory card or Shira. He'd know by now about the phone call

Ari received earlier. The little hairs at the back of John's neck tingled and he wished Colin would just spit it out, whatever it was, and then they could figure out how to deal with it.

"The man you knew as Paul Chen is dead."

"What?" Ari asked, her voice shaky with panic.

"Wasn't he in federal custody?"

"Yes, but someone got to him. When they did bed check he was lying on the floor. They took him to the infirmary, but it was too late."

John slid his hand over Ari's and gave it a gentle squeeze. She looked shell-shocked and after everything she'd already been through that morning, he wasn't sure how much more she could take.

"How did he die," she said, her voice barely above a whisper.

"We need to do an autopsy, but it was poison of some kind. Probably slipped into his food."

"Does this change anything?" John asked. Maybe Colin didn't know about the kidnapping. If he'd been dealing with Chen's death all morning maybe no one had been monitoring her calls.

"Honestly, I'm not sure. My boss called me

and said since he's dead and there is no proof that the Chinese MSS are behind it, the case is being dropped."

"Wait, how can they do that? What about all the threats?" Ari asked.

Her hand shook under John's and he wished he could make all of this disappear.

"I don't know. It's out of my hands. I'm hoping the CIA will pick it up, but for now, there's not much I can do. He pulled your protection a couple of hours ago without even telling me."

"What the fuck is that shit? He's just going to cut and run now? What about keeping Ari safe?" Now John vibrated, not in shock but anger. It took all of his willpower to stay in his chair and not get up and punch the wall or Colin.

"I know, believe me. I don't agree with this, but my hands are tied, it's above my pay grade," Colin responded and looked genuinely upset.

"But it's not over. I can't believe Paul is dead, but…" Ari stopped short of spilling every-thing from earlier, but it was too late by then.

"But what? Did something happen?" Colin sat forward and stared at Ari.

"It doesn't matter, Colin. It won't help you, and now more than ever you don't need to be involved. The FBI is closing the case so you should just walk away. I'll make sure Ari is safe." It wasn't how he operated and they both knew it. Colin might have to follow orders, but it didn't mean he liked it.

"Tell me anyway. I think I might need to take some vacation. It sounds like the perfect time to burn some leave."

John glanced at Ari and she nodded. Telling him everything was the right thing to do. Hopefully, he wouldn't lose his job.

"Before we explain, you might as well know that not only does my team know what's going on but so does my ex-SEAL boss, Chase. He runs a Security company based in Florida and I brought him in on this yesterday."

"Didn't trust the FBI?" Colin asked.

"Not really. Something seemed off about this whole mess. The missing phone for one. How does that happen? I know you didn't lose it."

"Nope, I didn't even know about it."

"I believe you, but only because I know you so well. But it set off a shit ton of alarm bells."

"Thanks, I think."

"I believe you too," Ari said. The color was coming back into her cheeks again.

He couldn't believe she hadn't had a meltdown yet. The woman had nerves of steel. "How about we go into the other room, I'll call Chase and we can try to figure this out. We had a development here this morning too."

"I'm not going to like it, am I?"

"Nope, I think you're going to be even more pissed off. It also makes me wonder if you've got someone playing both sides in your office."

"I've been wondering about that myself," Colin muttered.

CHAPTER 12

The phone rang exactly twenty-four hours later. Ari hadn't slept at all and even John holding her while she tried didn't help. Thoughts of Shira being hurt, or worse, was making her crazy. If anything happened to her it would be her fault, no matter what anyone tried to tell her. If she hadn't gotten involved with Paul none of this would have happened.

As the time for the call grew closer, she'd constantly checked the phone to make sure it was charged, and that the ringer was on full volume. She was so hyper-focused that when the phone finally rang, she jumped out of her chair to answer it even though it was inches from her hand on the kitchen table.

The SEAL team and Colin were all there. They'd brought over doughnuts and coffee to try to distract her, but she was still a big ball of nerves. Then they went over the plan for the fifty-millionth time. Ari knew it backward and forward but still wasn't convinced it would work.

Now that it was time to put the plan into motion, she was terrified. Not so much for her, but for Shira and all the guys. But they were out of time.

After John nodded that the trace was in place, she answered. He and Colin had headphones on and would be able to hear everything that happened on the phone call.

"Hello?"

"Do you have it?" It was the same heavily accented voice as the day before.

"Yes. I have it." She was lying and thanked God that they couldn't see her face. They had torn her apartment apart after they'd hung up with Chase's team and even with seven of them searching they hadn't found it. Instead, Chase helped John create a new one loaded with fake information Colin supplied.

"I knew you would find it. All you needed was the right incentive."

"I need to know Shira is okay." It had been one thing Colin stressed, that they needed proof she was okay.

"Do as I tell you and she'll be fine."

"I want to hear her voice again or I won't do anything." Demanding anything from the kidnappers freaked her out. She couldn't believe she'd made them do it yesterday but for some reason, today was scarier.

"I told you she's fine. You can see for yourself when you get here."

Colin shook his head 'no' and her stomach clenched. If she made it through the call without throwing up all over herself, it would be a miracle.

"I need to hear her voice." Ari's voice sounded wobbly and she knew he'd hear it. Not exactly the way to get what she wanted.

Silence first, then what sounded like an argument between at least two people. The sound was muffled, and they couldn't hear anything clearly.

"Or what? You'll have your SEAL take me out? You have no idea who you're dealing with."

The urge to tell him off was so strong she had to literally bite her tongue. She didn't give a crap who he was, and she knew as sure as she knew her name, that John would wipe the floor with him.

"I didn't tell him like you asked. So do this for me. Just let me hear that she's okay." Maybe pleading wasn't the best idea, but if they thought she was weak it would help her later.

More muffled voices and then the one she'd been praying for.

"Ari?"

"Shira, thank God. Are you okay?"

"Yes," Shira said, her voice weaker than usual, but it was definitely her.

"There, you have your proof. Now if you want to see her alive you'll do exactly what I tell you."

"Okay." Ari was so relieved the nauseousness she'd been struggling with subsided until he started talking again.

"Do you know where the old warehouse district is in San Diego?"

She did know it, and it was the perfect place to kill someone and never have their body found. Most of the buildings were closed down. "Yes."

"Come to the corner of Fourth Street and Market. Go with the man who approaches you and he'll take you the rest of the way. Come alone and make sure you're not followed. If we see anyone with you, your friend dies. If you tell anyone, your friend dies. If you don't show up, your friend dies. Do you understand?"

"I do. How long do I have to get there?"

"I'd suggest you hurry."

The line went dead and Ari took a deep breath and met John's eyes. As long as she focused on him, maybe she could hold it together.

"You did great," Colin said as he took off his headphones. "We'll get these sonsofbitches and Shira will be fine."

"I wish I had your confidence."

"It'll be okay, Baby. This is what we antici-pated. I don't like it, but you'll be wearing the tracker. My team is the best and we'll be watch-ing," John said as he massaged some of the tension from her neck and shoulders.

"Are you ready?" Colin asked, then he slid a

little plastic case holding a memory card across the table.

"Yes." It was a lie, but she would fake it until she got to Shira. It couldn't be worse than when she was arrested and put in jail. She'd never been more terrified.

"Don't forget, we have your six," Elwood the big SEAL team boss said from the doorway. "They'll never see us coming, it's what we do."

"I don't want you to get into trouble. You're not supposed to do anything on American soil." It had been one of the things bothering Ari since they'd come up with the plan the day before.

"We're not going to be doing anything. Colin will handle it once the police are involved. It'll be fine," John said. He'd spent most of the night before giving her a million reasons why it was okay for them to help.

Between Chase and his team, the SEALs, and Colin she couldn't ask for better back up. Too bad she was the weak link in this scenario. A few months of self-defense classes were probably not going to be much help when she had to deal with the kidnappers.

"Can I talk to Ari alone for a minute?" John asked.

"Make it quick, the clock is ticking," Colin answered pointing to his watch. Then he left with the SEALs.

"I know you're scared. I'd be worried if you weren't. But we'll be close even if you can't see us. You need to trust me."

"I do, more than anyone, but there's so much we don't know. What if there are ten people there and they shoot me as soon as I show up."

"They won't, they'll want to make sure you have the memory card first. That will give us the time to get there."

"Okay." Ari's insides were jelly, but it was time to suck it up. Big girl panties or not, she had to save her BFF and make sure no one else got hurt. She could do it. Maybe if she kept saying it over and over she'd convince herself.

"Good girl. In a couple of hours, this will all be over, and I'll take you out for a wonderful dinner, just you and me."

The woof from under the table reminded her that Mr. Darcy wasn't going to be happy being left behind either. But no way was she bringing her dog to a gunfight. Just thinking that made her almost giggle.

"Okay, you too Mr. Darcy. But you have to promise no stink bombs," John said with a laugh. He was so calm it helped her nerves.

"Thank you."

"Don't thank me until after dessert." The waggle of his eyebrows made her smile. They hadn't done more than kiss and cuddle, but the electricity between them was incredible. She'd never felt like this with anyone else.

Pulling her into his arms, John tilted her face up and rubbed his lips against hers. What started as a gentle kiss, quickly turned passionate as his tongue slid into her mouth and dueled with hers. Her hands wrapped around his neck as she melted against him.

If it hadn't been for Colin clearing his throat who knew how long they'd have stood there. But it helped. For those precious few moments, she'd forgotten about everything else.

Part of the plan was to act like she had to evade John and the FBI protection detail. Since they weren't sure what surveillance the kidnappers had on Ari, they didn't want to take any chances.

The FBI team had been reassigned, but Colin parked his car in their usual spot to make it look like they were still there. John was to take Mr. Darcy for a walk so she could 'sneak' out of the building.

Grabbing her purse, she put her phone and the memory card inside. She had a tracker on her phone, and another sewn into the collar of her shirt in case they made her leave her phone behind. Knowing there was a backup made her feel a little better.

"Ready?" Colin asked after John and Mr. Darcy left.

Instead of the elevator, she took the stairs. By the time she got to the bottom she promised herself she'd do more cardio if she got through the day and was more than thankful she only lived on the fourth floor.

Adrenaline pumped through her veins and she'd broken out into a sweat before she'd gotten to the first floor. Turning right instead of left, she went down the hallway to the maintenance exit. After double-checking that no one had seen her, she opened the door, ran across the back alley to the next street and grabbed a cab. An Uber would have been better, but she didn't know if she had the time to wait.

The next sixteen minutes were the longest of her life. Every traffic light became her enemy. They hadn't said how long she had, just to hurry. They'd better not hurt Shira because she was taking too long. When the cabby finally pulled up in front of Market and Fourth she breathed a sigh of relief.

After paying and stepping out of the cab, she stood at the corner of the building and looked around. Panic started to set in as she waited. Had it taken her too long? Had the man given up on her? Her body had cooled in the car and her clothes damn with sweat make her shiver. Door-to-door had taken exactly twenty-six minutes with the added time to get out of the apartment building and grab the cab.

In the cab, she'd taken her phone out of her purse and shoved it down her side inside her underwear. If they searched her, maybe they wouldn't feel it there. Even with the second tracker, she'd feel better if she was able to keep her phone.

Checking the time on her watch, she wondered how long they'd make her wait. Attempting to look like she was resting against the side of the building, she looked around hoping to see at least one of the SEALs. Nothing. They'd said they were good, and she believed them, but it would have been nice to know for sure they were there.

The waiting was horrible. Visions of Shira being tortured kept flashing in her mind. Sweat broke out on her forehead and the breeze made her shiver. Worrying made it worse and if she had to stand there much longer she was probably going to throw up. Before she'd finished the thought, she was grabbed from behind and a cloth doused with something stringent was placed over her nose and mouth. As much as she struggled, she couldn't pull away before everything went dark.

CHAPTER 13

John got back to the apartment with Mr. Darcy. Everyone else was gone, so far the plan was running like clockwork. Quickly changing clothes he strapped on his ankle harness then added his shoulder harness. U.S. soil or not, if anyone tried to hurt Ari he would take them out. Ready to join the rest of his team, he grabbed the keys to his truck and ran into a fuzzy wall blocking him from the door. Mr. Darcy stood in front of the door with his leash in his mouth.

"You can't come, boy. It's not safe." Instead of moving away, he got closer to the door. The only way John was going to get by him was to pick him up and move him. It's what he should have done but bringing him might not be the worst idea. If they lost the trackers, he'd bet his life that the dog would be able to find Ari. Then again, if anything happened to Mr. Darcy, Ari might kill him.

"Okay, you can come, but you need to listen to me no matter what. Our girl will kill me if anything happens to you." The wagging tail and loud woof were enough for John. He put the leash on, and they headed to his truck.

After he got Mr. Darcy settled, he connected the Bluetooth and called Colin.

"I'm on the way, where am I headed?"

"The signal is coming from a warehouse on Ninth Street. We're on J Street about six hundred feet away."

"Thanks, I'll be there as soon as possible. I wish we could hear what they're saying."

"Me too. But the tracker just stopped moving."

"If you get a bad feeling about something, don't wait for me, just go and get them."

"I planned on it. Just get your ass here."

"Copy that," John said and looked over at Mr. Darcy. "It'll be okay." He wasn't sure if it was to reassure the dog or himself.

The building was huge, run-down, and had four entrances. Too many to easily do reconnaissance and not be seen. The SEALs had staked out each of the doorways while waiting for him to get there.

"I think we should go in and get them. I don't like waiting. It's not like she can give us a signal."

"Disco just reported back that the building is wired with explosives. If we breach they could detonate the bombs and implode the building."

"So what then? We stand out here and wait until we know they're both dead? I don't like this. We don't have eyes or ears, just a little blinking light."

"Don't go into that building."

"Or what? You'll arrest me? Seriously, the plan was to go in as soon as she was with Shira. What changed?" John didn't like the look on Colin's face. He was up to something. Running two separate missions was not cool, especially if it put Ari in danger.

"I need to make sure that the guy behind this is inside. It's the only way to stop it. There has to be a mole in the FBI and catching one of

Chen's contacts will be the only way to figure it out."

"I don't give a fuck. That's my woman in there. You may think she's collateral damage, but I don't."

They might have been friends fifteen years ago, but this was total bullshit. It's why he hated working with the alphabet agencies, they always had an ulterior motive, and he'd hoped that Colin was better than this. But he could piss up a tree for all he cared right now.

Using his coms, he contacted his team. They were going in to save the women.

It was dark and smelled worse than any fart bomb Mr. Darcy let loose. Unable to see anything, she had no ideas where they'd taken her. As she tried to move, whatever they'd used to restrain her cut into her wrists. It was the same when she tried to move her legs.

It was so quiet she couldn't tell if she was alone or not. Maybe Shira was there but couldn't speak. She couldn't even tell if they'd found her phone or if the tracker was still in her collar. Now she understood why John had tried so hard to come up with something where they could talk to each other. But Chase convinced him it was too risky. It sure would have been nice to hear a friendly voice right about then.

"Ari?" It was barely a breath of sound, but hearing it was a huge relief.

"Shira?"

"Shhh. Don't move. They think you're still unconscious. Move your finger if you understand."

Ari moved the fingers of both hands; not sure which side Shira could see from her position. So grateful that her bestie was alive she had to restrain herself from firing off a bunch of questions.

"They took everything you were carrying, and then when they searched you they found your phone. They weren't gentle when they did it either. One of the guys was pretty pissed for some reason."

"Great."

"Shh, what did I say?"

If things weren't so dire, she'd probably laugh. It was typical Shira tossing out all kinds of comments and questions and not letting her answer. It sucked that they found her phone, but hopefully the tracker on her shirt was still working. She was ready to get the hell out of there, so she was fine with the SEAL team showing coming to their rescue.

"The bitch is awake." Okay, so much for luck. Time for Plan B, only problem, she didn't have a Plan B, at least not yet.

"Good." That was the voice of doom from the phone conversations. She decided it couldn't hurt to make a case for releasing them.

"I think you should let us go. You have my purse, which means you have the SD card you wanted. We are nothing to you. I'm blindfolded I can't even identify you." A sudden burst of bright light blinded her temporarily. So much for not being able to identify them. Slowly her vision returned as her eyes grew accustomed to the light. They were in a huge open loft that was still under construction.

Shira was restrained in a chair on Ari's right side. She was horrified when she saw her bruised and swollen face with rivulets of blood down her cheeks. Ari's eyes filled with tears.

"I'm sorry."

"Shut up, you twat, did anyone tell you to speak?" Asshole. He needed to be kicked so hard in the balls they lodged in his throat. Just thinking about how satisfying it would be to do that, made her realize she wasn't scared. What she was, was pissed off. They roped her into this and taken away her control, now she'd do her best to make them sorry. Hopefully, John and the 'cavalry' showed up before she ran out of ideas.

"What are you going to do, kill me?" Maybe that wasn't the best question.

"It would be my pleasure, bitch." Dirtbag number one punched her in her right cheek. Pain, stars, and lights out.

Ice water made for a rude awakening. This time when she opened her eyes, she was face-to-face with the dirtbag asshole who'd punched her. Too bad she couldn't move her feet. It would have been nice to kick him in the balls so hard he'd have to get them surgically removed from his windpipe. It made her smile, and that wasn't the best idea. The guy lifted his fist and she winced as she anticipated another punch, but the other man, who seemed to be in charge, stopped him.

"No. I need her alive for now." Saved by the voice of doom from the phone. Wonderful.

"You son of a bitch," Shira yelled.

As Ari watched in horror, dirtbag asshole number one kicked Shira's chair. She screamed as she landed on the floor with a loud thud. "That's what you get for interfering, bitch."

Then he turned back to Ari. "Ms. Nelson, do you want to be the reason your friend dies today?"

No, she didn't, but she had to find a way to stall for as long as possible to give John a chance to get there. She could see five dirtbags but there might be more. Without knowing how long she'd been unconscious there was no way of knowing when the SEALs would bust in to save them.

"The micro SD card is in my purse. You don't have to hurt her, I brought what you asked for."

"You mean this one?" He held a small memory card in front of her face.

"Maybe? They all look the same and I didn't see where you got that one." Her answer earned her a slap from the voice of doom, and dirtbag one used a bat on Shira's left leg. Her screams echoed through the loft. Ari gagged. She was helpless to do anything while they beat Shira. Praying that John would get there soon, she didn't know what else to do.

"I got this from your purse but it's not the card Chen gave you. Don't even try to lie to me, we know what was on there. He'd already showed us. We need that card."

"My bad."

He didn't like her response and it earned her a punch in the stomach from dirtbag asshole one. It took her breath away and she gasped in pain. Thank God they hadn't hurt Shira that time. Her bravery was wearing thin, and she didn't know how much longer she could maintain it.

"I don't think you understand the severity of your situation, Ms. Nelson. No one knows where you are, and they'll never find you unless you give me the memory card."

"And then what? You'll kill me quickly?"

"Yes, and leave your body in one piece so they can identify you." That didn't sound all that wonderful, but the first option scared the crap out of her. She definitely couldn't handle torture. Why hadn't John gotten there yet? Was it possible that they'd been caught and were dead?

Shira was whimpering in pain and Ari didn't know how to help her. She didn't have the damn micro SD card and didn't have the first clue where Paul had put it. After yesterday, it's not like she could ask him either.

"Are you going to cooperate?"

"I don't have the card. I don't know what you're talking about. Paul never gave me anything. If I knew where it was I'd give it to you."

"That's not good enough." Voice of doom said in a voice dripping with ice.

Knowing it was coming didn't help. It only made her tighten up in anticipation. This punch was harder than the last one and it knocked her chair backward and her head connected with the concrete floor and then everything turned black.

Ice water revived her. How long had she been unconscious? What was it with these guys? Did they really think she was holding back when they had her tied to a chair and beat the crap out of her?

"I don't have it," Ari said through chattering

teeth. Shock was setting in. She'd read about it and at this point, her body couldn't deal with much more. From her position, she couldn't see Shira. The only proof her friend was still alive was her soft moans.

It was starting to look like there was a good chance she was going to die and never see him or Mr. Darcy again. A tear mingled with the remnants of the water they'd poured over her and dripped down her face. The tears weren't for her, they were for Shira, Mr. Darcy and John. All of this was because of Paul. Everyone she loved was suffering because of him. Why did he have to pick her?

Anger burned hot inside her shivering frame, she needed to hold on they had to pay for what they'd done.

CHAPTER 14

Planning the rescue was nothing new for SEAL Team Charlie. They gathered around John's truck and discussed the intel they had. Their earlier plan had Ari being rescued as soon as her tracker went steady. The fact that Colin didn't give the go order infuriated John. This was his woman, and who knew what the motherfuckers were doing to her.

Elwood mapped out the plan, they didn't have their full gear but did have their IR goggles and were armed with their knives and sidearms. There would be hell to pay unless they could prove self-defense, but each team member agreed to the risk of operating on American soil.

Gus, Disco, and Shaggy headed over to the roof of the adjacent building. From there they'd repel through the top floor windows. Colin shared the information he'd gotten from a drone IR scan and it would have to be sufficient.

"This scan was done ten minutes ago, it's the most up-to-date intel we have. It looks like the women are located on the third floor in the rear right quadrant," Colin said as he read the information from his phone.

"How many targets?"

"There are six heat signatures besides the women. It looks like there are two on the first floor and two on the second. The other two are near the hostages."

"No one on the roof? Or upper floors?" Elwood asked.

"Not when we got this, we will have another report in about thirty minutes," Colin replied.

"Thirty minutes will be too late," John said, barely containing his fury. He'd settle this with Colin later and it wasn't going to be pretty. It blew his mind that he'd been willing to take chances with Ari or Shira's lives.

After his own near-death experience, he'd learned not to take anyone or anything for granted. Especially not a life. It also taught him that if you want something, you need to go for it. And he wanted Ari. He'd spend the rest of his life proving it to her if necessary.

The other members of Charlie Team looked as pissed off as John. Even though he'd been with them for less than a year, part of their survival counted on being able to read each other. Whether Colin realized it or not, by deciding to put the women in danger for the sake of the case, he'd made some enemies.

With the new intel, they had a better idea for their breach. As usual, the plan changed.

"Okay, we change the plan," Elwood said. "Gus and Disco you clear the first floor. Me, Riot, and Shaggy will take the second floor. We'll rendezvous in the stairwell. Go in quiet. No guns. We don't want to tip them off."

"Copy that," the Team said in unison.

"Colin, you stay here and let us know if anything changes. This time no holding back," Elwood said, his voice deceptively calm.

"Will do."

"Questions? Concerns?" Elwood asked before giving the order to go.

"I want them alive. We need to find proof of the mole in the FBI," Colin requested.

It was the last thing John cared about. Doing the job was one thing, but he'd overstepped this time, even though he understood Colin was only doing what he thought was right.

John handed Mr. Darcy's leash to Colin. "We'll do our best, but I'm not making any promises. The hostages come first." He stared at him almost daring Colin to object. But he nodded as he took the leash. "Mr. Darcy, stay here. I'll bring our girl back soon."

It should have been all that was necessary, except Mr. Darcy had his own plan. Pulling his leash out of Colin's hand, he ran after the SEALs.

"Fine, you can come, but you need to listen, and be quiet, no woofing and definitely no stink bombs, got it?"

"You do know you're talking to the dog like it's human?" Disco said.

"I know, and half the time I think he's a human in dog form."

Like clockwork, the team found their targets and took them out without making a sound. Executing the next part of the plan would be more difficult since they didn't know the condition of the women or their captors.

As they assembled in the second-floor stairwell, they were riding high on adrenaline. Disco had even found the detonator they'd placed on the first floor and disabled it.

"All clear?" Elwood asked.

"All clear," they repeated back.

"If the third floor is laid out the same, we should be able to breach here, stay against the walls and take them out."

"And if that doesn't work?" John asked. He knew what he wanted to do, but he'd promised to try to keep the bad guys alive.

"Make it work, we need them alive," Elwood replied. "Do you copy?"

The team acknowledged the order. As they made their way up the stairs, an ear-piercing scream came from the floor above. If it wasn't for Shaggy's hand on his arm, he'd have run up the rest of the stairs and blown whoever was up there to bits.

Taking a deep breath and focusing on the mission instead of Ari's face, he nodded, and they continued their ascent. Mr. Darcy stayed at his side and he prayed the dog would follow orders even if he spotted Ari.

As they passed through the open doorway, the dog didn't make a sound and stayed with the SEALs as they moved around the outer perimeter of the large room. The building was part of the revitalization project, but the work hadn't begun.

Gus and Elwood came up behind the two tangos as they were arguing in what sounded like Mandarin. None of them spoke it, but John had studied it and recognized some of the words. Unfortunately, not enough of them to know what they were yelling about.

The kidnappers should have been more aware of their surroundings, but it made it that much easier for the SEALs. Gus grabbed one of them and held his ka-bar to his neck, while Elwood took out the other one. They'd managed to take them both alive. But where were the women? John yelled for Mr. Darcy to find Ari and the dog practically galloped across the open area.

The dog led him to the two women who'd been left behind a stack of boxes on the far side of the floor. Now he knew why they hadn't seen them after they'd breached. When John caught a glimpse of Ari's face his heart almost stopped. Shira didn't look any better.

There wasn't an inch of her face that wasn't covered in bruises and dried blood. The left half of her face was so swollen she was unrecognizable. But it didn't stop Mr. Darcy from trying to comfort her. Whimpering, he licked her face a couple of times, but when she didn't respond, his crying grew louder.

Praying they weren't too late, John kneeled by Ari's side and checked for a pulse. "She's got a pulse. It's weak but it's there," John called out, his relief obvious. Grabbing his knife he cut through the plastic ties to free her from the chair.

Before he could go to Shira to cut her loose, Disco had already released her. "She'd not doing well, looks like she's got a compound fracture, both of them probably have concussions. We need to get them to the hospital," Disco said as he checked Shira for open wounds.

Ari was still unconscious, but Shira moaned when Disco cut her free from the chair.

"Shira? Can you tell me where you're injured? I want to move you," he said.

If he hadn't known for sure it was Shira, he'd never have believed it. Of the two of them, she'd been beaten much worse. When she finally answered, her voice was barely audible. She'd been full of life when he'd met her on Friday and now she sounded like a lost child.

"My leg is definitely broken, not sure what else. They punched me in the face a couple of times too."

"Definitely a concussion," Elwood said after he'd made sure both of the tangos were properly secured.

"Ari, Baby, can you hear me?" John was afraid to touch her.

Trying to remain calm when the woman he loved was lying broken and bloody on the floor, took all the willpower he had. He couldn't get her to respond to his voice or light touch and her skin was cold and clammy. It terrified him.

Mr. Darcy looked up at him and whimpered and then nudged her with his nose. He didn't get a response either. But that didn't stop him. After the third time nudging her face and licking her check, Ari finally opened her eyes.

"Welcome back, Baby." John's relief was

palpable. Seeing her eyelids flutter and open allowed him to breathe again.

Mr. Darcy licked her face and she smiled. If he hadn't been watching he'd have missed her lips move but he couldn't hear her. Leaning close, he kissed her forehead gently.

She whispered, "I knew you'd come. My white knight..."

To say Ari's memory was fuzzy after the attack would have been a colossal understatement. Not that she was complaining. She'd rather forget the beating they'd given her, just the memories of pain and ice were more than enough. Besides, her body reminded her every time she moved.

When she'd woken up in the hospital, she'd been thoroughly confused and had a hard time remembering much of what happened. Her body reminded when she attempted to sit up in the hospital bed. The excruciating pain in her chest and the pressure and pain in her face filled her eyes with tears.

"Easy, Baby, you were banged up pretty

good. You will need to take it slowly for a while."

She hadn't even noticed John had been sitting next to her bed until then. Closing her eyes, she tried to remember how she'd gotten to the hospital. It was like a fuzzy cloud hiding her thoughts. Then she remembered Shira lying on the cement floor.

"Is Shira okay? I want to see her." Panic filled her voice and she tried to get out of bed again.

"She's right here. We asked the staff to put you in the same room. See?" John stood up from the chair and pulled back the curtain dividing the two halves of the room.

Shira really was sleeping in the other bed. Thank God. Tears rolled down her cheeks and onto the front of her hospital gown, as guilt replaced relief of knowing she was alive. Would her BFF ever forgive her?

"Is she okay?" Ari whispered, not wanting to wake her friend.

"She might disagree with me but yes, she is okay," John answered.

The beating Shira received had caused a lot more damage. When she'd tried to escape they'd used a baseball bat and broken her femur in three places. It took surgery to put her leg back together. Her leg would never be the same but at least she didn't lose it. He'd found it interesting too that Disco had been hanging around waiting with him.

"Thank God. I thought they were going to kill us."

"Colin is going to need to talk to you when you're up to it. I told him I'd let him know. He wasn't too happy, but he can get over it."

Ari hadn't heard John talk about him like that before and she wondered what happened while she'd been unconscious. Before she had a chance to ask, her doctor came to check on her.

"Glad to see you're awake. Could you step out for a bit while I examine my patient?" Dr. Hernandez asked John.

"I'll be right outside if you need me."

"She'll be fine. I promise," the doctor said with a chuckle.

When they were alone the doctor smiled before starting his exam. "He's a very dedicated boyfriend, he hasn't left your side for more than a few minutes since you were admitted. He even gave them hell in the ER when they wouldn't let him into triage."

"He did?"

"Yup. You have a nasty concussion, but we needed to repair your fractured cheekbone," Dr. Hernandez said as he lifted a light and moved it back and forth in front of her eyes.

"I guess that's why my face hurts."

"Excellent powers of deduction, Ariana. You also have three broken ribs."

Now the pain she'd felt when trying to sit up by herself made sense. "I'm having trouble remembering what happened."

"I'm not surprised. The concussion is probably the main cause, but you were under a lot of duress. Sometimes our brains shut down to try to protect us. I think as you continue to heal, most, if not all of your memory will return. I'll give you a card for a neurologist. If would be a good idea to make an appointment to be checked as you start healing."

"Thank you. I appreciate that. It seems strange to have holes where I know I should have memories."

"I'm sure. Try not to push yourself too hard. If you find you're getting a lot of headaches you should make an appointment as soon as possible with your doctor."

"Okay. So when do you think I'll be able to go home?"

"Unless something changes, I'll write your discharge papers for tomorrow. But you have to promise to take it easy. You have *at least* six weeks of recovery ahead of you to let those bones heal."

"I will."

"I'll stop by to see you before you leave. Be well, Ariana."

"Thank you, Doctor."

After the doctor left she was annoyed at herself for not asking about Shira, her face must have shown it since John looked concerned when he came back into the room.

"What happened? Did he give you bad news?"

"What? Oh no. I got great news—I can go home tomorrow. But I forgot to ask him about Shira."

"Don't be, he wouldn't have been able to tell you anything unless you're listed as her POC."

"Then how do you know so much? You're not related to me or my POC," Ari asked.

"Because Colin was able to find out about both of you since it's an open FBI case."

"Wait, wasn't the case closed? Maybe I'm remembering wrong."

"It has and it hasn't. It was supposed to be but since we were able to catch the people behind Shira's kidnapping it's open again. Whether or not he'll be able to prove espionage, I have no idea."

"I remember getting to the warehouse but not much else."

"Did you ask the doc about it?"

"Yeah, and he said it would probably all come back."

"Great, see, like I told you, nothing to worry about. I'm glad they're discharging you. Mr. Darcy has been inconsolable."

"Aww, poor Mr. Darcy. I miss him too. Wait, was he at the warehouse?"

"He was. I wondered if you'd remember that. It's kind of ironic but he kissed you awake. It should have been my job."

Ari tried to grin at the hurt look on John's face, but the shooting pain in her cheek brought tears to her eyes. She might not be able to smile, but it didn't stop the warmth that flowed through her body and filled her heart with joy. It was like they were a little family. "You'll have more opportunities, I'm sure."

"Promise?"

"Yeah, that's one promise I can definitely make."

CHAPTER 15

Elwood and the rest of the team came by to visit Ari and Shira later that afternoon. It took about five seconds to see that Disco was definitely focused on Shira. John decided to give him a break, for now, since he'd been the only one not teasing him about Ari.

Shira was awake when they came in and John introduced her to them.

"It's nice to meet you. And I can't tell you how grateful I am that you saved us. Those fuck-tards needed an ass-kicking. I hope you gave them a good one."

"We sure did," Disco replied as he moved

closer to her bed. "How are you feeling. They sure did a number on you."

"It feels like it, but it could be worse."

"I really appreciate everything you did for us. I hope you didn't get into any trouble," Ari said.

"We're fine. Colin made sure it was all covered," Elwood answered.

There was something about the way he'd said Colin's name that made her wonder if something else happened. "Hey, where is Colin?"

"He'll be by later. I know he has some questions for you," John answered.

"Is everything okay?" Ari asked. It seemed weird.

"Everything is perfect, Baby."

The guys stayed until the nurse came in to do their vitals and shooed them out.

"I'm going to go for a bit and take Mr. Darcy for a nice walk now that you're doing better. I'll be back in a couple of hours. If you need anything, either of you, give me a call." Then he leaned down and kissed her on the forehead.

John couldn't have been happier that Ari

was going to be okay, but he still had to deal with Colin. Elwood had calmed him down when they first got to the hospital, but the more he thought about it the madder it made him. Sure Colin had a job to do but getting the women out of there should have been his first priority.

As he walked through the parking lot toward his truck he saw Colin pull into a parking spot. If he was smart he'd walk away, but that wasn't his strength, he'd always been an all-in kind of guy. No reason for him to change now.

For an FBI agent, Colin's reflexes were damn slow. John had him up against his car before he even knew he was there.

"Give me one good reason why I shouldn't beat the shit out of you. Or at least break a few ribs like the women in that hospital are dealing with?"

"I don't have to justify myself to you. You shouldn't have been involved in the first place."

"And you were the one that brought me in. Are you sure you want to make me more pissed off? I swear I'd happily go to jail right now for the satisfaction of beating you to a bloody pulp. Those women are going through hell and it's because you didn't send my team in like we'd agreed."

"I made a judgment call. I know you don't agree with it. It was my OP and my decision. I feel bad that they were hurt, but it was worth it all to get this espionage pipeline to China shut off. And if I'm lucky, I'll uncover the mole in the FBI too."

"I should put your face through this window. I can't believe we were friends. That's over from this minute on. You put the woman I love in mortal danger and it was unnecessary. If the team had gone in sooner you'd still have the same evidence you have now."

"Not necessarily and if you want to play it this way, then fine. But it still comes down to I had a job to do and that outweighs any one person. You know damn well you've dealt with the same thing on missions."

It took every ounce of willpower John possessed to restrain himself. That and the security guard that pulled up.

"Is there a problem here?"

John backed away from Colin and turned to the guard. "Nope, no problem here. Right, Colin?"

"Everything is fine, thank you for checking."

The guard hesitated a moment like he wasn't sure if he believed either of them, but then he continued on in his golf cart.

"If you know what's good for you, you'll apologize to those women before you question them. There may come a day when I can rationalize what you did, but it's not this day and won't be anytime soon. If you're smart, you'll stay away from us for a while."

Colin shook his head. "They'll both have to testify. It took some fancy wrangling just to keep you and your team out of the report. If you were smart you'd be thanking instead of threatening me."

John shook his head and walked back to his truck. There was no getting through to him. He had a dog waiting for him at home and a woman recovering in the hospital. Getting thrown in jail for assaulting an FBI agent was not the smart thing to do.

They were resting when Colin visited about an hour after the SEALs left with John. Ari wanted to know what was going on between him and John but figured it might be better if she didn't ask. Instead, she and Shira listened as he explained that they charged the two men with espionage as well as kidnapping and attempted murder. He even apologized for their injuries but explained that they had done a good thing for their country.

Ari wasn't sure everything they'd been through was worth it, but at least Colin was happy. The man she'd called the voice of doom had a name—Chen Fui. As far as the FBI could tell, he'd been Paul's handler and was probably the one behind his poisoning. It didn't look like he'd give them much information, but Colin was still hopeful.

After Colin left, Shira shifted in her bed to face Ari. "I don't blame you. You need to get over yourself."

"What?" Like always it was as if Shira could read her mind. Ari had been blaming herself the whole time Colin was talking. Her friend should never have been pulled into her mess.

"Who do you think you're kidding? I've been your bestie for how long? You're sitting there feeling horrible because I got hurt. Well don't. You didn't kidnap me or beat me. That asshole dude did."

"Dammit. But it is my fault."

"No, it's not. If we're going to play the blame game, it's that dick Chen that started all of this. If he hadn't come into your life nothing of this would have happened. And as horrible as it sounds, I'm not sorry he's dead.

Ari wasn't sure how she felt about Paul's death. He'd lied to her from the beginning, gotten her arrested and almost killed, but she felt sorry for him. Maybe he'd been forced into spying, maybe they had something over him, or threatened his family in China. She'd never know for sure. "I kind of feel bad for him."

"Holy shit, girl. Whatever. Either way, none of this is your fault. I love you and I don't want your guilt driving a wedge in our friendship. Especially not when you're going to have all these great SEAL stories."

"You're terrible, you know?"

"Yup, I do, and that's why you love me."

"You're right. I do."

"I need a nap," Shira said as she leaned back and closed her eyes.

Ari smiled. The room seemed a little

brighter and the tension in her shoulders eased a bit. Maybe it was a new beginning for her. She was going to enjoy giving John shit for deceiving her when they first met. But she couldn't be mad, not after everything he'd done for her, even if she wasn't quite ready to let him know yet.

As promised, Ari got her discharge orders and John came to spring her from the hospital. After a teary goodbye with Shira, she promised to visit the next day. She couldn't wait to get out of there even if going home didn't mean to her apartment which was still disaster central and she'd be staying with John for a while longer.

Before she let John help her into his truck, she lifted her face to the sun and tried to take a deep breath of fresh air until the pain in her ribs stopped her. For the first time in over a year, she didn't have to worry about what might happen. No one was following her or watching every move she made. It was more liberating than she'd have believed, and it put a huge smile on her face. It hurt like hell, but it was worth it. Six weeks of healing for her broken cheekbone sucked, but it was nothing compared to Shira's recovery time.

"I have a surprise for you."

"I'm not sure I'm up for any more surprises," Ari said, but then she saw Mr. Darcy. "You brought him. Thank you, thank you. I missed you so much."

John said he explained to her dog that she was hurt, and he'd have to be gentle with her. And in true Mr. Darcy fashion, he gently licked the non-bandaged side of her face. His tongue was soft as silk.

"Thank you. My two favorite men and I'm out of the hospital. This day is simply amazing."

"You ain't seen nothing yet," John said with a chuckle as he gently clicked her seatbelt into place. Mr. Darcy climbed into the back and leaned his head over her seat as if to keep an eye on her.

It didn't take long to get to their building, and as the elevator doors opened on their floor, Mrs. Laramie was waiting for them. How she knew when she'd get home, Ari had no idea, the woman always seemed a little magical.

"Welcome home, dear. I'm so glad your young man kept you safe. And your Navy SEAL too," she said with a wink and handed her a vase filled with beautiful flowers.

Ari gave him a sort of half-smile. Oh yeah, John was going to take lots of ribbing from her friends too, he had no idea. But Mr. Darcy was the hero of her story, he'd even had his picture taken for the newspaper. Who knew he'd be so famous. Thankfully, he was still the same loving, Sir Fartsalot that she knew and loved.

"Thank you, Mrs. Laramie. It's good to be home."

"If you need anything let me know. I'll bring some cookies over later."

"Thank you, that's so sweet. I love your cookies." She tried to hug the old woman gently so she wouldn't break the fragile octogenarian or hurt her own ribs. But she wasn't very successful. She couldn't believe how much pain her ribs were causing, almost more than her face.

Following Mr. Darcy and John to his apartment, when he opened the door she was greeted with streamers, balloons, and more flowers. He'd decorated the living room for her homecoming, and it brought tears to her eyes. He was a keeper. She'd gotten more than lucky this time and she wasn't stupid enough to let him get away.

"I can't believe you did this for me."

"Baby, I keep telling you that I'll do anything to make you happy. I'm in love with you."

Mr. Darcy danced around in a circle wagging his tail as if to let her know he helped. Reaching over she fluffed his fuzzy head and then pulled John's face toward her so she could give him a thank you kiss.

"Wow. That's the first time *you* kissed me."

"It is not."

"Yes, it is. The other times I kissed you."

"Well, I guess I'm going to have to remedy that."

"Oh yeah?"

"Yeah." She sat on the couch and pulled him down with her and winced from the sharp pain from the broken ribs.

"Dammit, be careful. Those are going to take a while to heal."

"I know. But I need to talk to you."

"Uh oh."

"No, uh oh. I've had a lot of time to think, and you were right about a lot of things."

John opened his mouth, but she put her finger across his lips to keep him quiet. She knew what was coming and she wanted to get it all out before he interrupted her.

"All the stuff with Paul wasn't my fault, and I wasn't stupid, or reckless. I'd been played by a pro." She stopped and thought for a minute before continuing. "I didn't want a relationship because Paul was my first long term boyfriend. I thought what he offered was real, but it wasn't. I see that more clearly now. You've shown me what caring is in so many ways and not empty words. Because of you, both Shira and I are alive. And Mr. Darcy loves you and don't they say animals are the best judge of character. You've really grown on me over the last year and I want to see where this takes us."

He opened his mouth, then closed it, then opened it again. "Does this mean what I think it does?"

"Yes. You've proven that happily ever after's can happen, and it doesn't have to be a knight on a white horse. A Navy SEAL and a fuzzy dog are much better."

John gently lifted her onto his lap. She gazed into his gorgeous green eyes and sighed. Yup, this was happiness. Then he kissed her so gently his lips were like butterfly wings against hers. It amazed her that it didn't matter how passionately he kissed her it still curled her toes and sent her heart racing. No, not happiness, it was love.

I t wasn't until two weeks later that Ari was feeling well enough to tackle the mess that used to be her apartment. The crime scene tape had been taken down over a week ago and a new door installed. Until you opened the door, you'd have no idea that there was a disaster area on the other side.

"Holy crap, I'd forgotten just how bad this is," Ari said with a loud sigh and then she giggled. "You know, I look about as bad as this place."

"No, you don't. Your face looks a lot better now."

"That's not what the mirror says."

John rolled his eyes. "Can you believe her, Mr. Darcy?"

The dog looked at each of them as if to say, "You humans talk too much. Get to work."

"You know, we don't have to go through everything today. There's no rush unless you're sick of staying with me?" John said with a fake pout.

Sick of him? Hell no. She was actually kind of dreading moving out of his place. Not being around him all the time would be hard. He brought sunshine into her bleak life, and she'd fallen head over heels for him. Waking up in his arms from her nightmares, taking Mr. Darcy on long walks, and watching movies every night.

They'd created a life together without even trying and that it was coming to an end. Just the thought of no longer sharing his life dimmed her sunshine. But she couldn't assume he wanted her to stay. He said he loved her, but he hadn't said anything about the future.

She'd talked about it with Shira when she visited her every day. They both wondered what he was thinking since he hadn't brought up the future at all. Shira said she should come right out and ask him, but that wasn't Ari's way. She'd give him a bit more time to see if he really wanted a life with her.

Their only disagreements had been about Colin. John was still pissed at him, but Ari understood why he made the choice he did, even if she didn't like it. She just wanted to put it all behind her and move on and that included going back to work. When her boss called and told her they'd kept her job open, she couldn't have been happier. Once she was cleared to return to work, life would finally get back to normal.

"Where are you going to start?" John asked as he stood in the middle of the mess that used to be her living room.

"Not in here, that's for sure. I think I'll go work in the bedroom. This way I can grab more clothes. I'm getting sick of wearing the same thing every couple of days."

"Okay, Mr. Darcy and I will start in the kitchen. But you need to take it easy. No stretching or reaching. Sit in the chair I left in there, and I'll bring you what you need."

"You don't have to be a mother hen. I'll be good."

"You'd better."

"I will," she said and blew him a kiss.

"Mr. Darcy, maybe we can find something to eat."

"You just had breakfast."

"And your point is?"

Shaking her head, she stepped carefully over the debris on the way to her bedroom. It was weird being back, the last time she'd been there had been the day she found out Paul died. It seemed like it had been months instead of weeks. Her life had changed so much. The swelling was almost gone on her face, but it still felt strange. Hopefully, after another four weeks, she'd be fully recovered. Wincing as she pressed a hand against her still tender ribs, she sat down in the chair John left in the bedroom.

John and Shaggy had taken most of the furniture to the dump to make room for the new stuff she'd ordered. It wouldn't be coming for another couple of weeks, so he was right, they didn't have to do it all in one day. Most of what was left were the items that made the apartment hers—clothing, photographs, her kitchen stuff. Most of it had been broken or was ruined, but she found the photo of Mr. Darcy from the first day she'd brought him home and miraculously it was unbroken. As she rubbed it against the sleeve of her shirt to clean it off, the edge of the wood broke off.

"Hey, look what I found," she yelled to John.

"What did you find?" he asked from the doorway.

"Mr. Darcy's adoption day photo. But I think I just broke it cleaning off the fingerprints. It is one of the few things that survived the dirtbag brigade."

"Let me see, if I can't fix it, we'll just get a new frame."

She handed it over and he ran his finger along the edge where she thought she'd chipped the wood. Instead, a little door popped open revealing a micro SD card.

"Holy shit, it was here all the time. I can't believe it," Ari said as she took the little card from John.

"You had this when you were with Chen?"

"Yeah, but it had a picture of the two of us that he got for us on our first anniversary. I liked the frame, so I kept it and put Mr. Darcy in it instead, he's prettier."

"Woof."

"Yes, you are."

He rubbed against her legs and she leaned down gave him a kiss on the head. "I should call Colin. It looks like he's going to get his mole after all."

"Yeah, I guess so.

"This is a cause for celebration. Can we go to Amici's tonight for some lasagna?" Ari asked, trying to get John to smile after her mention of Colin. It was sad their friendship had been destroyed. But she still had hope that they'd work it out.

"Sounds perfect."

John gingerly pulled her into his arms and smiled. "You are the love of my life. I know it's too soon, but when you're ready, I want to marry you. You have erased the darkness I've lived with since I was injured. I give you my heart, my body, and everything I am."

Tears welled up in her eyes and spilled down her cheeks. He was her dream come true. The man of her fantasies had become her reality and she'd go through it all again just to end up in his arms.

"I love you too."

His lips rubbed against hers, enticing her to open. His tongue swept her mouth and rubbed against hers. Her toes curled and her body tingled with desire. She couldn't wait for her damn ribs to heal so they could finally make love. But until then she'd be content to stay wrapped in his arms.

"Damn, Baby. You're killing me. How much longer until those ribs are healed? I want all of you."

Ari gave him one of her crooked smiles. It was funny that they were both thinking the same thing. "The doctor said about four more weeks."

"Shit. I don't care what else is going on, but four weeks from today, I am taking you to bed and we will be there a while," he said with a huge smile.

"No objections from me," she said as she stared into his beautiful green eyes. "As long as I'm with you, I'll be happy anywhere."

Mr. Darcy woofed.

"And with you, Mr. Darcy, always."

It had been a hell of a year, but when Ari called to tell him that she'd found the SD card everything had been worth it. He'd rushed over to her apartment, after all this time he didn't want to wait any longer to see if he could uncover the FBI mole.

It took the IT guys a couple of hours to unencrypt the card. He'd been pacing back and forth for so long he was surprised he hadn't worn a path on the floor. When they finally got it unlocked and opened the files, he couldn't have been more surprised. Everything that had been fucked up suddenly made sense, and he couldn't have been more pissed off.

Placing a call to the director, he sent the contents through encrypted email. It didn't take long for him to get the go-ahead. Taking two other agents, they went up to his boss's office and knocked on the door.

"Guess what we finally found?"

Special Agent in Charge Richard Landau looked up from behind his desk. He must have seen something in Colin's eyes because the color drained out of his face.

"What did you find?"

"The missing SD card. How could you betray your country like this? You almost got Ariana and her friend killed. Hell, did you kill Chen yourself?"

"You don't understand…"

"No, I don't, and I don't actually care. You're under arrest, you have the right to remain silent…"

As Colin watched the other two agents lead his boss away in handcuffs he finally breathed a sigh of relief. He doubted he'd ever understand how Landau had turned, the betrayal he felt rocked him to his core. But at least he'd been stopped, and he could close this chapter. For now, it was time for a celebratory drink.

The End

Thank you for reading *A Soldier's Temptation*. I hope you'll check out the other books in the Beyond Valor series. If you enjoyed this story, please leave a review.

Thank you,

Lynne

xoxo

ABOUT THE AUTHOR

Lynne St. James has been writing for as long as she can remember. She has series in romantic suspense, contemporary, new adult and paranormal. She lives in the mostly sunny state of Florida with her husband, an eighty-five-pound, fluffy, Dalmatian-mutt horse-dog, a small Yorkie-poo, and an orange tabby named Pumpkin who thinks he rules them all.

When Lynne's not writing about second chances and conquering adversity with happily ever afters, she's drinking coffee and reading or crocheting.

Where to find Lynne:

Email: lynne@lynnestjames.com
Amazon: https://amzn.to/2sgdUTe
BookBub:
https://www.bookbub.com/authors/lynne-st-james
Facebook:

https://www.facebook.com/authorLynneStJam es

Website: http://lynnestjames.com

Instagram: https://www.instagram.com/lynnestjames/

Pinterest: https://www.pinterest.com/lynnestjames5

VIP Newsletter sign-up: http://eepurl.com/bT99Fj

Music under the Mistletoe – A Raining Chaos Christmas
(Novella)

Tempting Flame

Anamchara

Embracing Her Desires

Embracing Her Surrender

Embracing Her Love

The Vampires of Eternity

Twice Bitten Not Shy

Twice Bitten to Paradise

Twice Bitten and Bewitched

Want to be one of the first to learn about Lynne St. James's new releases? Sign up for her newsletter filled with exclusive VIP news and contests!
http://eepurl.com/bT99Fj

Made in the USA
Columbia, SC
01 April 2022

58317672R00164